RTHENGER

^{THE}RiNGER

GREG HUNT

Matador
9 Priory Business Park,
Wistow Road,
Kibworth Beauchamp
Leicester LE8 0RX, UK
Tel: (+44) 116 279 2299
Fax: (+44) 116 279 2277
Email: books@troubador.co.uk
Web: www.troubador.co.uk/matador

ISBN 978 1848767 027

British Library Cataloguing in Publication Data.
A catalogue record for this book is available from the British Library.

Typeset by Troubador Publishing Ltd, Leicester, UK

Matador is an imprint of Troubador Publishing Ltd

Printed in Great Britain by the MPG Books Group, Bodmin and King's Lynn

For Siân, Toby and Jocelyn.

ACKNOWLEDGEMENTS

Siân, thank-you for all your support during the making of this book. You have been the unwavering tenor keeping the ringing sounding out whilst Toby and bump have been happy distractions throughout.

To my wider family, enjoy!

To all those that I have rung with, it has been a pleasure; from Thurcaston to Portsmouth Cathedral to Reading to Kidderminster and now Alvechurch. What a wonderful hobby it is. My life seems to have revolved around campanology; from friends, to my dissertation, to outings, to this novel. We're still raising money for the 'new and refurbished' peal at Alvechurch, so for more information please visit www.alvechurchbells.org.uk

To my ringing mentors over the years, Eric Atkinson and Richard Pawley, Stuart Heath and Richard Harrison, Helen Priest and David Struckett and to David Macey, thanks for the encouragement and some good striking, may you never clash!

To my parents who decided to follow me into the art, there have been some treasured moments ringing with you – keep it up. To my brothers – one day you will succumb!

To the La Plagne Ski Beat crowd from the 2003/2004 season – the location was my inspiration for the Alpine adventure – what a great time we had.

To many of my university colleagues and ski crowd – yes, your names were taken in vain but this is a work of fiction and, apart from the names, there really is no connection.

Lastly but by no means least to the Troubador team for making the dream of producing this book a reality.

Happy reading!

CHAPTER 1

The helicopter gunship's blades reverberated around the high altiplano in the heart of the Bolivian highlands. The dawn sunrise was spectacular and the air was still. Any sound carried far across this barren arid landscape with its snow-capped mountain ranges.

The 4x4s on the ground, an ageing mix of Toyotas and Nissans, skidded to a halt. The salt crystals under their wheels flew across the Sal de Uyuni, a vast expanse of salt lake close to the tourist centres of Potosi and Sucre. These towns were more commonly known as gateways to the Andes, and provided access to this vast untouched environment.

The driver of the lead vehicle had been grinding the coca leaves around his gums, desperate to stay awake until the dawn. His two passengers had succumbed to the need for sleep. As foreigners to the dry high plains of the altiplano, they were unaccustomed to having half the oxygen that each took for granted at sea level.

Scrambling for his CB radio, the driver spun the vehicle and pressed the accelerator to the floor. It was soon to be fully light, and the white, camouflaged vehicles, hurriedly snaking their way across the salt plain, were now visible from the skies.

On the horizon, one of the many cactus covered brown islands in this desert wilderness rose up from the white salt plain.

The island started to edge closer as the wasp-like humming of the helicopter's swooshing blades became not such a distant din, audibly rattling towards the escaping

1

convoy. The sun had edged above the horizon, allowing the island to cast long shadows across the salt hexagon pavement. The exposed vehicle train was hurriedly carving the distance to their safe area.

'Boom!' The second vehicle in the convoy skewed to the right, the inside tyre fragmenting. The occupants, the driver and passenger, looked up in horror as a dark, low shape appeared on the skyline. The three vehicles behind did not stop. The 4x4s tyre had blown, and driver and passenger were in trouble. The driver had pulled out an old fashioned pistol and his colleague scrambled out of the passenger door.

The helicopter crew had long been watching for any sign of movement across this section of the altiplano. It had been a normal, uneventful shift. The machine was soon to turn back as, at such heights, fuel did not last long. A glimmer on the endless salt plain attracted the observer's attention. There were lakes that glimmered, but this was too small for a lake. He signalled to the pilot and the gunship smoothly descended into the Sal de Uyuni valley, like a cobra preparing to unleash its deadly load.

The first vehicle had hidden itself behind the island, which provided a stark contrast to the flat and featureless landscape. The huge white tarpaulin disguised its shape. It also provided cover for the remaining three vehicles. All members of the convoy helped with the last loops of the tarpaulin. There was a deathly hush.

The driver of the second vehicle knew that his pistol was no match for a helicopter gunship. He raised his arms in the air, the eponymous vision of surrender.

The helicopter had become a roar above the salt plain, the shape of the craft creating a shadow flying along the brown side of the Andes mountain range. The observer identified the stranded vehicle and the pilot twitched the joystick accordingly. The helicopter screeched and groaned as it banked across the sky. The passenger was running across the salt flat, the cold was stopping him from sweating, but his face had drained of blood and started to mirror the colour of the ground below him.

The pilot depressed a switch on the side of the joystick. Three seconds later the driver and vehicle on the high altiplano had been obliterated. Flames curled upwards to the light blue sky. The shocked passenger continued to run for his life, scrambling off the salt flat, desperately looking for cover, but there was none.

The observer opened up the barrel of the sidewinder. It only took twenty seconds to hone the accuracy of the helicopter's formidable weaponry. An eerie quiet descended on the Sal de Uyuni as the sound of the swooshing blades slowly faded away.

CHAPTER 2

Archie Malcolm climbed the spiral stone staircase to the ringing chamber. There were fifty five steps but it always felt like there were more.

He was in good shape and bounded up the narrow, dark space, past the small vertical slit openings, which gave a tantalising framed view onto the naval port below. The heavy set ringing chamber door creaked open at his insistent push and he dropped down the couple of internal steps onto its floor.

"Grab hold for a touch of Grandsire Caters," bellowed the Tower Captain. "Morning Archie. How about you take the fourth?" Archie felt honoured to be part of this Cathedral group. Over the next ten minutes all of his troubles went away. He thought about nothing else except for the ringing, remembering his place, ensuring that he was striking the bell as well as he could and once again proving himself a reliable member of the band.

The ringers finished their touch. The Tower Captain put the clock chimes on and the tenor rang out like a deep base drum announcing the eleventh hour of the day. Over four thousand towers across the United Kingdom had bells that were being rung that morning.

The bells remained in the up position, balanced against their wooden stays like upturned mushrooms. Any would be liable to fall, given a pull of the dangling ropes in the ringing chamber, heavy passing traffic, or an earthquake type event. The Tower Captain motioned to Archie that he had to attend to the flag on the roof for the Queen's Birthday and he needed to climb up through the bell chamber.

Both Archie and the Tower Captain scrambled up the faded silver metal ladder leading from the ringing chamber, through the musty bell chamber to the roof access hatch. Breathing heavily, the Tower Captain prised open the locking pin of the heavy hatch and hauled himself onto the lead lined roof sheet.

As the much younger man, Archie manoeuvred himself more gracefully, and helped to unfurl the tower's flag. A cool breeze ran through the stone masonry and caught the cotton material holding the Queen's colours.

Whilst the Tower Captain was hoisting the flag, Archie quickly scanned the edge of the dockyard with his keen eyes. There was not a better view or a higher perch in the whole of historic Southsea. As he had guessed, the colourful fishing boat, the *Alana Princess*, was just pulling off beyond the dockyard and she was clearly heavily laden. She ploughed through the water, heading across to Ryde on the Isle of Wight.

Archie raced down the ladder, excusing himself in a throaty shout to the Tower Captain for PhD studying, and slipped down the spiral staircase, past the organ, and out into the hustle and bustle of Old Portsmouth.

Ten minutes later a young, athletic man strode purposefully through the main gate of HMS Dolphin, where the sentry on duty saluted to his superior. He crammed the documents, that were attempting to escape, back into his dark leather holdall. He swiped his pass card against the door entry system on the side-wall, marched through the door into an open-plan seating area and hung his coat on the wall.

Monica glanced at him dismissively. The young man glared back.

"Please go through," she said.

The double doors opened electronically. The soft padded floor and red leather armchairs were shaded away from the grey, tinted, half-shuttered blinds. The long mahogany boardroom table was surrounded by a number of occupied chairs. A gravelly voice rose up from the man at the head of the assembled party, "Ah, Lieutenant Malcolm, you have decided to join us."

CHAPTER 3

Lieutenant Malcolm took his seat at the mahogany boardroom table. He was hot from rushing out of the Cathedral and gulped the sparkling mineral water that lay in the glass in front of him.

Commander Edgar Bennett took a long, deep intake of breath, whilst unconsciously curling the end of his thick moustache, and then spoke authoritatively, in a voice that demanded respect and focused all of the participants to listen expectantly to his resonant tones.

"We are all aware of the increased sophistication that is being used in the trafficking of illegal goods into our waters. We need to take further measures to ensure that the routes are closed down, the perpetrators brought to justice and the trade brought to an end. A message has to be sent back to the traffickers that the United Kingdom will not tolerate smuggling of any kind and that all illegal cargo will be seized immediately and destroyed."

There was silence in the room. The occupants at the boardroom table resigned themselves to the current position, their shadows detailing postures that had slumped. The United Kingdom was on the back foot, smuggling was easy. The establishment's lack of resources meant that the island was seen as a simple target, the ample coastline an easy end destination for narcotics and illegal immigrants.

Malcolm shifted in his seat and Bennett had noticed his eager expression.

"Malcolm, if you are attempting to say something, spit it out."

Malcolm rose to his feet. He needed all the time he could muster to compose himself and to think logically.

"We have been tracking a fishing boat called the *Alana Princess* and request permission to board her when she next docks at Ryde, which should be in fifteen minutes. We are led to believe that she carries a full cargo of narcotics and her seizure will be a valuable breakthrough in stemming the cocaine trade to Portsmouth."

"Good," Bennett replied. "Let us focus on some small wins to lead us to the bigger fish. You are relieved to board and capture any illegal goods on the vessel and I want a full report."

"Yes sir," Malcolm replied, as the electronic doors were already swinging open. He winked at Monica, to her disdain. He grabbed his coat and swiped the push button to exit, walked hurriedly out of the main gate and onwards towards the naval dockyard.

The boarding team at Ryde received Malcolm's message. Their GP14s were slung over their shoulders as they climbed up from their rubber inflatable and athletically straddled the guardrail that stood proud above the bulky grey hull of the *Alana Princess*.

The first man headed straight for the bridge and nudged his loaded gun into the generous waist of the Captain.

"Show me your manifest," he demanded.

With the gun in such close proximity, the Captain was quick to co-operate. The scrawled sheet detailed a hold full of white bait, herring, diesel, rope hemp and netting. The other three men of the boarding crew were already descending into the hold, their headlamps casting eerie contortions of light that bounced off the metal hull of the fishing boat.

Nearly three quarters of an hour later it was apparent there was nothing to capture. The boarding crew reported to Malcolm. Malcolm reported to Bennett. This was an embarrassment. "A pointless exercise," Bennett replied.

CHAPTER 4

North of Cuzco in Peru, close to the start of the Machu Pichu tourist trail, the llamas and alpacas were being herded along the narrow winding track.

The animals did not complain. They shuffled along at a hypnotic pace. Each beast still had its warm winter coat despite the beginning of the snow melt. It would soon be late spring.

Four herders accompanied the twenty seven animals. These were local tribal men who knew the mountains well. They preferred working with the animals than having to farm lower down the mountain, or within the cramped silver mines, or the pittance that they could earn from working on the coast among the non-tribal Spanish colonisers.

The route would take them from the Urubamba river, past the Inca ruins of Llactapata, over the high pass of Warmiwanusca at 4,200m and down past the more impressive Inca sights at Sayacmarca, Puyupatamarca and Winaywayma. The herders would then hand over their precious cargo at Machu Picchu.

The 4x4s had off-loaded the crates for the tribal men to pick up earlier that day. The vehicles had been late. The quantity of crates was seriously reduced. A fifth of the expected boxes had not made the journey from Potosi through to their rendezvous north of Cuzco. The 4x4s had covered a formidable thirty six hour route of Andean wilderness and rough, hard tracks.

The animals were making steady progress on the difficult walking ledges. Much of the path had been previously cut into the side of the mountainside and to the edge of the pathway lay steep, formidable drops. The animals just followed the leader and, every couple of minutes, the beige llama at the head of the procession gave off a tinkle of noise as its neck bell clattered against its glistening fur coat.

It had been raining hard over the last few days. The herders had been surprised by the unusual conditions and still led the llamas and alpacas, wearing poor leather sandals. The animals were each weighed down by the crates tied onto their backs. This added the weight of a small adult to each of them. The head llama reached a steep and narrow gulley in the path and let out a small snort. The closest herder whacked his stick against the animal's hind quarters and she stumbled forward again, leading her twenty six fellow beasts onward.

The herders were tired, having enjoyed their last evening before working. The local lager *cusquena* had been acquired from a friend's tourist stall at the heart of Cusco and had featured strongly on the previous evening's menu. Their responses were slow.

The lead herder saw the rocks start to slip above the animals only after the first five llamas had begun to straddle the path within the gully. He ran to push the beasts back to the safety of the non-moving path behind them.

He was pushing the beige llama as she lost her rear footing and a large boulder crashed into her, taking the animal down the gulley. The landslide had begun to gain momentum and there was nothing that the second herder could do, except watch, as a further four of his beloved animals and his cousin were thrown down the gully and over two hundred metres to the valley floor.

CHAPTER 5

Archie Malcolm changed to a lower gear and swung out to overtake the long vehicle that had been holding up his progress. He had the top down of his Mazda MX5. His friends joked that it was a hairdresser's car. Well, he wasn't quite a hairdresser, but it was his affordable fun and this was his day off.

He nipped in front of the HGV, now rapidly disappearing in his rear view mirror, and smiled. He was close to singing to the CD mix collection he had been compiling over the last few weeks but since he really could not sing, he hummed along and put the volume up a notch.

The Downs came and went as Archie hummed along to the eighties pop music he liked so much. The chalk cuttings cast a swathe through this beautiful rural landscape and enabled the little Mazda to make quick progress up to the M4 and onwards West over the Severn Bridge. He paid the toll to enter Wales but then headed north, destination Ross on Wye.

Archie had been invited to a close friend's birthday and Emma was going to be there. Clearly, it was important to be at his friend's party and support David whom he had known since school, but the reason that he had been humming so well was because all he could think about was Emma.

He could not remove the vision from his mind. The fun and energy, the lovely locks, the style and sophistication yet hands on approach to life. They had been friends for the last couple of years through David, yet he so wanted more.

This helped to make the drive fly by. All those invited to the birthday party were to be Canadian canoeing at Symonds

Yat on the River Wye. In the back of his mind Archie was thinking that if he couldn't woo Emma Canadian canoeing, with a warm up drink with the rest of the crowd afterwards in a comfortable hostelry, with a roaring fire burning, then he might as well give up. With his background, Archie was a dab hand at outdoor pursuits, but always the gentleman, very modest with it. This was his real chance, doing an activity where he really would not have to worry about anything and could leave his attention on only one thing.

He turned off the main A-road that he had been following for the last thirty minutes and wound the car down into the valley of the Wye. Surrounded by woodland, it was a peaceful, tranquil setting. A wonderful break from the frantic comings and goings of the last couple of weeks. His operational agenda was buried deep away from his current thoughts.

David, the birthday boy, stood tall and was wearing a party hat that had somehow been made to fit over his canoe helmet. He was surrounded by a mixed crowd of friends and relations of all ages and laughed in amusement as someone slapped his wetsuit cladded posterior with the back of a paddle blade.

As Archie pulled up close to the birthday party group he spied Emma standing on her own, her hair flowing in the breeze and catching the dappled light. Archie caught a lump in his throat and looked down slightly.

Emma played mixed-hockey each week. It was at her hockey practices that she had noticed a very talented hockey player who was athletic and funny. He always had people hanging around him of both genders. They seemed to be attracted to his invisible magnetism and enormous sense of humour. Emma was also affected by his warmth and character. He was a vital member of the team and never missed any practices or matches.

She had gone on to befriend David over a number of weeks and it was when she stopped round for a quick cup of tea after a hockey practice session that she first met Archie.

Plucking up his courage, Archie waved and to his joy Emma and David waved back simultaneously. Then Archie's phone rang; it was Commander Edgar Bennett. Archie's smile evaporated and his waving hand fell to his lap. He took the call and listened intently.

The Commander confirmed his worst suspicions. "We need you to report in immediately, Lieutenant. There have been developments."

CHAPTER 6

Commander Edgar Bennett looked at Lieutenant Archie Malcolm with a pained expression. "You're late," he said.

Archie nodded and gazed directly at the Commander, waiting for the important work that was to be thrust at him, having been pulled away from Emma. No doubt the birthday party group were well on their way down the River Wye, relishing the activity and drinking in the scenery.

The word "late" took Archie straight back to his school days in the Navy CCF. This Combined Cadet Force gave him a free insight into the world of the armed forces. At tax payer's expense, Archie undertook sailing courses in the Firth of Forth, mastering helming the *bosun* dinghies under the Edinburgh road and rail bridges. Near Poole Harbour in Dorset he went on to understand air acquaintance. He had liked the roar of the Sea King helicopters and, from Liverpool, he was able to go to sea in a naval *Frigate*. Archie had become adept at identifying the ways and laws of the sea and, in his spare time, he had studied and studied to understand more.

In his final year at school, Archie was able to meet with the Navy Schools Liaison Officer. This meeting took place on the third floor of one of the many old Victorian red brick buildings that were at the school.

Archie had been playing football during the lunchtime break and all his concentration had been on driving his team forward to ensure that they won the friendly match. Whilst it might have been called a friendly, Archie was in no mood to lose easily. He was prepared to keep running, keep tackling and generally be in the way of the opposition until his side won. Meanwhile, the Liaison Officer in his third floor room within the Victorian red brick building noticed that Archie had lost track of time.

Even though Archie entered the interview room, by his account, bang on the dot of when he should have been there, the Navy Officer let Archie know that punctuality was a core ingredient of the armed forces. He was told that he would not last long if he was late again. It was a lesson that he had tried to remember.

The Commander continued. "Archie, I want you to spearhead the naval taskforce in our fight against illegal imports, especially the growing cocaine trade through our waters and onwards to a sophisticated distribution network. It is currently a blight on our borders and I want you to take full control to curb this activity."

At last, this was exactly what Archie wanted, some measure of responsibility. An active assignment where he could take the lead and not just be another dogsbody, following in the footsteps of whichever boss was chosen for the task at hand. He hid his surprise.

"You do realise the current minimal resources that we have at our disposal, sir?" Malcolm clipped out.

"For the next six months Archie," the Commander sighed, "You will receive whatever reasonable and justifiable support you deem necessary."

CHAPTER 7

Since going to University, Archie had fallen in love with bell-ringing. A funny thing to fall in love with. A specialist activity you would think, but in terms of his alternative role in the armed forces it had always allowed him to be anywhere in the country. He could discreetly investigate what he needed to and the pastime provided cover throughout the day and evening for his daytime and nocturnal activities.

He had found campanologists to be a mixed bunch as a whole. Like so many pursuits, only men took part until the mid-twentieth century, and he could well believe, as he had been told, that not long before then every ringing chamber had a barrel of beer easily accessible to the ringers.

The image of the leather sandal, beer barrel bellied and bearded, middle aged man and his secretive hobby had moved on, but to be a campanologist was still a pastime not fully understood. The exercise was still viewed as secretive, with its societies and guilds, and many of the inner groups were by invitation only.

Archie, with his innate sense of rhythm, natural team playing abilities and dedication to hard work, did not take up the challenge lightly. If he could take forward a new activity, he always wanted to excel and this was particularly the case with this new hobby. A mix of physical exercise, rhythm, memorising of patterns and an ability to be aware of what all the ringers in the tower and their respective ropes were doing, Archie quickly caught on and proved himself to be a natural.

Most ringers would take a year just to learn how to handle the bell and be fully competent with their rope. The two part motion would involve being in control both at hand-stroke, by catching the fluffy "sally", and then also at back-stroke by holding the "tail end" of the rope. At back-stroke, most of the rope whirls itself into the bell chamber, wrapping itself around the wooden wheel, and Archie had developed a mastery of these basic two elements to have full control over all the bells in the tower within a couple of months.

Furthermore, normally, progression by way of rounds to call changes and then to method ringing would take the average ringer years. Archie grasped the harder methods extremely quickly. His analytical mind and perfect rhythm meant that he had picked up some of the complexities of the more challenging ringing methods within a couple of years. He had recently achieved a complex peal of spliced surprise major rung on eight bells and was currently working towards similar of royal, rung on ten bells.

The ringing band at Portsmouth Cathedral were rightfully proud of Archie and had brought him into the very heart of their group. He had been part of the recent striking competitions held within the Winchester and Portsmouth Diocesan Guild and, whilst not winning this year, he had rung as well as any of the ringers. He had gained their trust and confidence and this was extremely useful to him.

CHAPTER 8

The docks at Lima in Peru were run down. They would have appreciated being torn down, the materials recycled and a fresh new port being created. Obviously impractical and, for a poor country, definitely not possible. So the seafarers of South America and further afield made do with what they had.

The port of Lima was a place that you did not want to stay for any length of time.

This suited Natalia just fine. People in Lima were not aware of her and she did not care about them or anyone that she did not need to know. For those people that needed her and for those people that she needed, Natalia was one to watch in every way.

Natalia was the youngest daughter of Lima's mafia boss, Helis Morales, and what Senor Morales said was done. He had his fingers in all of Lima's money-making pies. The tourist trade was a major money-spinner for the Morales family. Senor Morales had made a wealthy living, successfully ripping off many of the tribal peoples of Peru who sought to sell their leather wares, shawls and alpaca or llama goods in the department stores and growing mini-shopping malls at the centre of Peru's capital.

These goods would have to travel large distances down from the Andes Mountains. The tribal people were not aware of the value of their wares in Europe and the US and, even though they believed they were receiving a fair price, Senor Morales had the contacts and the distribution network to triple the value of these beautifully made and very collectible items.

The leather wallets, bags and belts sold quickest. The market for alpaca shawls and fleeces was rapidly increasing. Senor Morales and his organisation owned the market, ran the market and did everything in their organisation's power to snuff competition. Any competitors were removed. Permanently.

Natalia enjoyed her work. She took delight in playing with other people's lives. She glowed warm inside when something she said could bring a look of horror, of animal fear, to a potential competitor. She would gain their confidence and use her sexual charms and flirtatious nature. Although she was not classically attractive, she made people stop and stare and it all helped when blackmailing the opposition. If the blackmail did not work, she talked to her brothers. Her brothers took pride in looking after their baby sister and, if Natalia made a request, they enjoyed seeing it through. Family values were important to the Morales. The kindred spirit ensured none of the Morales let each other down.

So, in full knowledge of the Morales's family reputation, it was with trepidation that the tribal men now stood in the 1970's dilapidated warehouse on the edge of Lima docks. The three had met the mule train further south at the foothills of the Andes mountain range. They now gazed intently at the tall Spanish lady, with dark, shoulder length hair, grey-green eyes and dark red lipstick. It exaggerated the slight sneer with which she returned their attempt at eye contact.

"You have not brought all of the packages that we requested you bring senores, why?" Natalia walked close to each man and behind the back of each of them, clicking across the reinforced concrete of the warehouse floor in her impractical stilettos.

Their volunteered leader appealed defensively, "We understand that the Bolivian convoy was attacked by government forces, and that there was a landslide on the normal passage through the high Andes."

"What has this to do with me?" demanded Natalia. "We make an order, and we expect it to be delivered. If it is not delivered, or part of it is delivered, or it is not of sufficient quality, then there are consequences."

The leader bravely, or perhaps stupidly, stayed put, "It is not our fault that we have delivered to you only part of what you have ordered, senorita. The matter has been out of our control and we require our normal payment for bringing the remainder of the order to you."

Natalia looked at all three men calmly and directly in the eyes, "I think you will learn not to cross the Morales family. This is an insult, and we do not like being insulted."

Natalia indicated to her elder brothers who had been standing in the shadow of the steel portal frame.

"Brothers, I need you to deal with these men," and she turned away and clipped across the warehouse floor, back into the dirt and grime of Lima docks.

CHAPTER 9

The beautiful mountain lodge was surrounded by fresh snow. The castellated ridges beyond had just caught the dawn and the tips had turned an incredible pink. The pink was similar to the pale flush of cold cheeks.

As the day began, the pink light descended down the breathtaking mountain landscape every couple of minutes. Slowly at first, and then slightly faster, the light crept towards the wooden chimney of the stunningly situated property, the only sign of human habitation in this very remote valley.

Any sounds would carry. Whilst at first glance the scenery might have been considered a poor habitat, it managed to support a surprising number of species. The marmot type rodents nibbled away at fallen bark, scampering across the snow at night, yet they always made sure they were back in their burrows before sunrise. The huge birds of prey adorning the rocky crags had panoramic views and used the air currents to move with ease. Occasionally, wild deer would venture up to these higher areas, but this was usually during the short summer season.

A light plume of smoke emanated from the top wooden chimney of the mountain lodge. A clear visible sign that the property was occupied. The lodge was indeed inhabited and, for the purposes of the French Alpine Authorities, this was just another holiday home being rented out.

The seclusion of this lodge was special, considering its general location within the French Alps. The neighbouring valleys contained much of the French winter skiing heartland. The resorts of La Plagne and Les Arcs, joined for the first time

21

in 2004 by a super lift called the *Vanoise Express,* lay just over the rise where the light had first hit the highest peaks. The nearest valley in the opposite direction held Les Trois Vallées with the popular favourites of Courcheval, Meribel/Mottaret and Val Thorens, with La Tania nestled at their base.

It was a beautiful spot. The chalet's privacy had allowed the man currently chopping wood in the small alpine forest, approximately three miles – or since he was in the Alps, five kilometres – from the mountain retreat, to carry out his duties over the last few weeks. His forehead started to perspire as he brought the axe down on yet another fallen trunk. His manner was no-nonsense. He wore walking boots which could strap onto snow shoes for moving across this terrain and the previous weeks had honed his physique. The walking boots were old-fashioned leather and his deer-stalker hat and overcoat, removed to chop the wood, gave him a hunter's appearance. He was middle-aged. The type of appearance where it would be difficult to tell if he was thirty-seven or in his early fifties, yet the alpine air and sun had weathered the hardy face. He had a distinguishable scar on his forehead and his forearms, now exposed since the removal of the overcoat, hinted at the power of the man.

He had brought along a flask, and a small rucksack held his sandwiches. The tranquillity and serenity of the surroundings meant that he was more than satisfied just gazing away from the edge of the forest to the landscape beyond. If he stood and climbed onto the pile of logs that he had chopped that morning, he was able to glimpse the Mont-Blanc massif. Mont-Blanc, at over four thousand eight hundred metres, was the Queen of the mountains within the French Alps.

For a hunter and wood-chopper he was extremely well equipped. In fact, the mountain lodge was a veritable electronic paradise. The ultra-modern, lightweight, small gadgets that adorned his temporary home meant that reception of any type of communication, despite being in the heart of the mountain range, was surprisingly clear.

Whilst day-dreaming, gazing at the beautiful view, his pager went off. Normally, a surprisingly piercing beep in the heart of this uninhabited mountain valley, thank goodness he had just set it to vibrate in his pocket. The screen was small but the type was clear: "Go to Code White". The Woodcutter picked up his snow-shoes and fastened them onto his old-fashioned leather walking boots. He trudged off back to the stunningly-situated, wooden mountain lodge.

CHAPTER 10

The Woodcutter in the French Alps extended his stride. The snowshoes meant he created little indent in the snow covering. The shoes were designed to spread his weight and make travel relatively simple.

The sun had now fully risen and, as the Woodcutter had already warmed up his muscles chopping the wood, he made short work of the distance back to the mountain lodge. It was an impressive set up. The height of the valley meant that there was permanent snow all year round. The lodge itself had been built into the mountainside with the basement and part of the ground floor tucked underground so that only the first floor with its windows and balconies stood above the ground.

The windows were covered in non-reflective glass and the snow that had fallen layered the roof and most of the surrounds in a natural white blanket. The property was extremely discreet and very difficult to find.

The basement areas had equipment stores with a couple of skidoos, hundreds of metres worth of climbing rope and related kit. This area of the lodge was an Aladdin's cave of outdoor equipment. Not only was there the standard mountain material of ice axes, crampons, winter coats, and thermals, but also skiing and boarding equipment to provide for the full adventurer's playground. The structural walls had also been modified, with exits leading above ground to allow for an escape, so that skidoos and other craft could leave the property extremely quickly.

The 'pièce de resistance' was the relaxation zone. Just up from the basement area, a pine sauna room and separate changing area, incorporating a shower, had been fitted, which led onto the Jacuzzi and small heated pool.

The main stairs from the basement lockers then led up to the ground floor, which held the communal seating area, kitchen and dining zone.

Adjacent to the leather clad seats, a wonderful wood-burning stove took centre stage with a large flue leading to the wooden roof rafters. The heat that the stove radiated was more than enough to warm the entire ground floor. When combined with the standard under-floor heating and radiators in each of the five bedrooms, it meant for a very cosy and hospitable chalet.

A discreet part of the chalet had been adopted for the Woodcutter's specific use.

Having arrived back at the chalet in double-quick time he had removed his jacket and deerstalker hat and walked up the main stairs to the first floor.

The second bedroom on the right-hand-side of the landing had no visible keyhole, no door-handle and no obvious seal or join. The Woodcutter had been proud of his work in setting up the alterations required and, after all, it was imperative that privacy was maintained if he wanted to continue to make a living.

He pointed an electronic fob at the reinforced steel opening. The steel was encased in wood to ensure an exact likeness of the overall effect of the chalet. It was important to his employers that everything continued to look 'just so'.

The door swung softly open, revealing an electronic paradise of computer gadgetry. All of the Woodcutter's work and his sole purpose in life lay within this communication equipment and the knowledge that it gave his employers.

His pager had indicated to go to Code White and he had been concerned by the news.

He had remotely turned on the main computer, prior to

entering the chalet. By tapping in the relevant passwords and double checking that there were no other frequencies or nearby communications being used, he was able to send his message. It was a simple message, but in sensitive code to ensure that no authorities would understand the name of the vessel. If it had been deciphered, the *Alana Princess* would have been in trouble.

CHAPTER 11

Below La Plagne in the heart of the French Alps lies a pristine small hamlet.

The height of the winter season was yet to pass in the small collection of chalets nestled together and hugged by the fresh, soft snow, lying a couple of feet deep.

Due to the newness of the snow, few tracks or indentations of any kind interrupted the white covering. The beautiful smoothness lay like a white, pristine duvet cover across this natural bowl, halfway down the mountainside.

The hamlet had retained its natural character, a couple of the mountain properties, originally farm out-buildings and summer mountain retreats, had been converted into sought-after mountain restaurants and expensive chalets. However, there were limited new buildings that straddled the snow covered, winding track that led to the centre of La Plagne.

Originally, the women of the Savoyarde region had been given those areas of land that were less productive, but where sheep could graze in the summer months. The men had always farmed the fertile land of the valleys. These lands remained snow free for most of the year.

The women had been the ones sitting on the potential goldmine. The mountainsides had proven themselves snow-sure, and with good gradients and travel links for tourists to come and carry out all manner of winter sports. Not only were skiing and boarding popular favourites, but this area was also a destination for parapenting. Aerial dare-devils would use the rising warm air currents to glide, dangling beneath a large aerial sail and gently manoeuvre themselves down to the valley floor. A sometimes hazardous activity as the air currents would frequently change, especially when close to the higher rock faces of the taller peaks.

The Olympic bobsleigh had also been constructed just below the hamlet and provided a destination for all different types of sleighs to rocket down the course, the ice bends twisting and turning to enable the sleighs to pick up enormous speeds.

There were also the alternative winter sports enthusiasts, who having skiied or boarded for years, trying their luck at cross country skiing, or husky dog sledging or at bombing around the slopes on the mechanical skidoos, used by the pisteurs to secure the safety of the pistes.

Others tended to admire the wildlife and stunning scenery, by using guides to go on snow shoe trails, and the general public could always just buy a pedestrian ticket to take one of the many gondolas up to the mountaintops, to admire the views whilst sipping a *vin chaud* from a perfectly placed summit restaurant.

Within the hamlet was one beautiful chalet named *Chalet Marguerite* and it had prime position within the small collection of wooden buildings. From its balconies, its residents could see all the way to the bottom of the valley. More practically, they could also check to see when the only chairlift leading out of the hamlet had opened, as the chairlift was situated opposite.

The chalet had one English family staying there this winter week and they were all accomplished skiers. They also knew the area and the resort well, having been coming to the region for a number of years.

The chalet was run by a South African couple who provided the meals and ensured that their guests were enjoying their holiday.

After a delicious breakfast of cereal, fresh baguette and

boiled eggs, the family soon prepared to go out and enjoy the fresh snow. They applied their sunscreen and ensured they had enough warm layers, before donning their ski-boots. Whilst the ski boot warmers had partially worked in drying out the boots, the family were experienced enough to ensure they did not breathe in whilst anywhere near the boot locker area of the chalet.

Heading for the chalet front door, the South African couple had already helped give out all of the lift passes and specific directions to the best slopes in the current conditions. All of the family were excited and their eagerness to hit the slopes was infectious. The South African couple were envious that the family were out for the first lifts and to enjoy the beautiful fresh snow, the first perfectly fresh snow that had fallen in the last week.

As the family were leaving, the chalet hosts asked to be reminded of their names and the parents confirmed theirs, the young men confirmed theirs and Emma, the Portsmouth University student, confirmed hers.

CHAPTER 12

The family crammed into the Grande Rochette gondola, which was busy as the fresh snow had also been spotted by many of the locals. As the lift pulled away, there was an air of expectation amongst all of the winter sports enthusiasts.

There were hushed whispers in a couple of different languages as the lift gradually ascended into the dizzying heights, seemingly unsupported, above the rock couloirs and gullies of the Grande Rochette.

It was an impressive set up, with the lift rapidly ascending over six hundred metres from Plagne Centre to the top of the rock massif.

In less than a couple of minutes, the whole family squeezed themselves out of the gondola car as it finally slowed down and gradually rotated at a slow, walking pace within the top lift station.

The young lads, each in their early twenties, were out first and went over to examine the piste map opposite the lift station. The view was impressive. A guide to the next group was pointing out Les Trois Vallées, which was clearly visible opposite, although a number of kilometres away, as the crow flies. On this perfect blue sky day all three of Courchevel's villages were distinct. The heliport was situated close by, increasingly being utilised by rich Russians as the resort had become a Russian favourite.

Emma's parents were tightening up their ski boots as Emma was warming up by jumping up and down on the spot. Fully prepared in her ski boots and skis, she was now sliding back and forwards. She really could not wait to ski down the inviting pistes and it had felt like an eternity since she had skied last year.

The family's warm up run, down a glorious red leading off the side of the top of the Grande Rochette and then onto a blue run towards Plagne Centre, had the whole family buzzing. The cool fresh air had blown through them all, awakening their senses and allowing their skis to move as one. The boys were out in front with Emma's mother trying to keep up with Emma's father, and her father was attempting to follow Emma just as she had started to *shus* to catch her younger brothers.

A couple of further ascents and descents and the whole family was ready for lunch. The exercise and cool air had meant that they were all ravishing, ready for some good food, and, in order to ensure that they were not dehydrated, both parents and the young adults were also looking for a fair amount of soft drink.

They found a corner table in the restaurant, next to a roaring log fire. The fire looked as though it had always been there, whatever time of day. It crackled as the family started to order in their limited French. The waiter appreciated the attempt, but soon the broken French requests for different, colourful, menu dishes took place in English. In no time at all the plates of Savoyarde specialities, featuring mainly cheese and potato based recipes, had been served and were being gobbled up by the hungry family of skiers.

All was well for Emma and her family and she was pleased to have such a wonderful break from her student studies. Her parents had enabled this to happen and she felt indebted to them.

Emma stood up. "If you have all had enough food, let's hit the slopes for some more fantastic piste action, the snow is too good to let it lie…"

CHAPTER 13

Whilst Emma and her family were munching through a hearty lunch in the French Alps, Archie Malcolm had co-ordinated his team and resources. He had a number of people reporting to him directly and, as Commander Edgar Bennett had confirmed, if he could justify it, then he could use the full force of the fleet and land forces.

The sniper hit the very centre of the target that was located over one hundred and ten metres from where he lay. A slight wisp of smoke blew across the range as the men took aim on the individual enemy targets. This test was important to them. Their Lieutenant Malcolm, respected and known as a strong team player, had confirmed that only full scores would be good enough. By this he meant ten perfect strikes on the centre bull and nothing less.

The look of concentration on each individual face said it all. The phrase 'a picture is worth a thousand words' is so often true and, just by looking at this team of crack professionals, you could tell that they wanted to be winners, to be a part of whatever mission lay in store.

Archie had not been able to tell any of his colleagues what they were competing for, where they would be going, or who they might be up against. It was just another perfect unknown for these soldiers and this was, after all, what most of them lived and breathed for.

The original sniper was onto his seventh perfect shot and the pressure was on. A tear slowly peeled out of the corner of his eye as there was a slight wind and, despite being close to the end of the summer, it was a little cool at six thirty in the morning.

The range was located just off Portsea Island, where access could be controlled through the double sentry manned gates and the one tarmac entry and exit road. Up to eighty snipers could be firing at the same time, using a variety of targets over different distances. Archie's eight hopefuls were firing their ten rounds over the longest distance with the smallest targets and Archie was enjoying it. He was willing them on. He wanted them all to be perfect and expected nothing less. His pacing up and down just behind their outstretched bodies was probably not helping his team to concentrate, but they were professionals and needed to deal with it.

As the marksman aimed carefully on his tenth and final shot, the cool air, which had allowed the single tear to roll down the bottom half of his cheek, started to make further progress downwards. It was one of those minor distractions, that is enough to irritate and put off the subject. The sniper blinked again and the single tear fell onto the top of the breach.

The pressure of the event meant that the sniper's hands were slightly clammy. By now he ached from having lain prone, partially supporting the weight of the rifle, with the barrel of the weapon nestled on the sandbags. The tear put him off. His shot went millimetres away from where it should have been.

He was angry, he knew that he was as good, if not better than the rest of this group and yet he had failed. A soldier with years of experience and combat and yet he could no longer put together ten perfect scores on the rifle range. An off day, a very off day. Not happy. Who to blame? Not himself, no. Who was the up and coming young officer who thought he knew it all? Archie Malcolm. Well, Archie Malcolm, you cannot have it your way all the time. You have to have some downs as well as ups and Petty Officer Stuart Betts will make sure that for once in your perfect life, Archie Malcolm, you will have a down.

CHAPTER 14

Emma's brothers were also keen to enjoy more of the fresh snow. They had recently purchased some of the new twin tip skis, which allowed you to land jumps backward without the skis digging in and, as a result, had become all the rage within the pro-riding skiing fraternity. Twin tips were also the standard ski seen in the board-parks, which were frequently being overrun by skiers who could perform all the tricks that boarders could and who were developing a couple more. The flying mid-air crossover trick performed using skis was a classic that the boys were perfecting.

Emma was not aiming to be a pro-rider, unlike her brothers, but she won on style. She could easily keep up with all their moves and could perform a trick or two herself. She was an experienced off-piste skier and, whilst she always tried to hire a guide when after new routes, she was very familiar with all the off-piste areas within the Les Arcs and La Plagne area.

Equipped with a shovel, expandable ranger pole and transceiver, as were her brothers, the three of them decided to head off the back of the top glacier in La Plagne – the Glacier de Bellacote. This would provide them with an exhilarating afternoon, and as the weather was fine with relatively low avalanche risk, the route would still be safe enough in the afternoon, being early in the season, with cooler temperatures.

The three students stepped out of the warm air of the restaurant into the fresh alpine day. All of the lifts in Plagne Centre were whirring away. A large queue was waiting for the Grande Rochette gondola as the lunchtime period was coming to an end. The refuelled skiers and boarders were making plans for the afternoon, and there was some jostling by the local ski school groups, who were already as competent skiers as most of the tourists.

Emma and her brothers bypassed the Grande Rochette queue and quickly hit their ski boots with their poles to remove any excess snow. Once the boots were clean, they were standing into their skis, front binding first and then slamming their weight down on their rear ski booted heels producing a reassuring click from the binding, once secure.

Clicked in, they schussed down to the chair-lift that would take them from Plagne Centre to Bellecote. Sam, Emma's youngest brother, did not schuss hard enough and as Emma and her brother waited to go onto the chair-lift, Sam had worked up quite a sweat by having to skate up the slight rise prior to the chair-lift queue. The lift operator appeared bemused and, in-between the chairs lifting off to float in mid-air, he was shovelling fresh snow across the ground of the chair-lift take-off point.

Nestled onto their chair, the lift machine allowed their piece of metal and seat cover to whoosh upwards with their feet dangling, momentarily, until Emma and her brothers wiggled their skis and robot-like boots onto the foot rests for the long chair ride up to the ridge overlooking Bellecote.

CHAPTER 15

It had been an exceptional season in the Alps, with a deep base in the snow levels being secured prior to the Christmas holiday season. The upper slopes had nearly three metres of snow and whilst the lower pistes were tracked, all of the runs within the Les Arcs and La Plagne Paradiski area were in good condition. The high level runs and surrounding areas lay untouched due to the relentless snow of the previous weeks.

Emma and her brothers were well aware of the conditions which meant that, now the sun was shining, there was a steady trickle of skiers all headed for the upper slopes, to make a mark on the untouched powder fields. The group headed past the entrance to the Olympic standard half-pipe on their approach to the resort town of Bellecote.

Emma's purple scarf caught the light breeze and fluttered out behind her, whilst her new atomic skis carved well through the fresh snow. Her skis were designed to be used fifty percent of the time on the piste and with the remainder away from the prepared snow ploughed areas.

Her brothers were attempting to outdo each other by skiing backwards at speed. Due to the nature of their twin tip skis a thin plume of snow was being emitted from the back end of the skis in a similar fashion to the arc of snow that is projected by snow cannon. The plume from each set of skis flew past the two students into the path of the snaking ski schools. These groups were slowly and carefully traversing across the steepness of the piste to make their descents for a late lunch or an afternoon tea in Bellecote.

As Emma reached the lower level of the piste near the exit

of the half-pipe, she gracefully executed a three sixty degree spin which slowed her down and brought her to a sliding stop, with a view directly upwards. The moguled piste rose to her left and she had an impressive view into the man-made, snow-built, aerial structure directly in front of her.

What had also caught her eye was the ability of the two skiers currently within the half-pipe, who had both performed two small aerial jumps. One of the jumps had been off the upper side wall with another completed by landing themselves onto the flat top of one of the sides of the pipe with a flourish of a one eighty degree spin.

Both of the skiers appeared to be of a similar age to Emma. Whilst she could not clearly see their faces, due to their goggles and helmets, they were athletically built and it was evident that both of the skiers had been skiing since walking age as they were so talented.

Emma could have watched and gawped for a while longer, she had felt an unfamiliar stir of emotion inside her, but pushed off quickly with her jet black, sleek, ski poles and descended down to the Bellecote Gondola, which would take her and her brothers directly to the summit of the Roche de Mio. At 2600m the Roche de Mio was second only to the Glacier de Bellecote within the La Plagne region.

CHAPTER 16

With the light breeze and sun shining, the top of the Roche de Mio was a wonderful place to be. Just behind the cable car station was 'Brown Trouser Ridge.' So nicknamed for obvious reasons, the narrowness of this castellated spur was barely enough for a pair of skis or board to perch, let alone allow the more daring to work their way along so that they could enjoy the magical couloir descents. These descents led into huge basins of untouched snow where, alone from the hoards for just a few minutes, one could inhale the majesty and real beauty of the mountains.

In the opposite direction lay the full megalith of the Mont Blanc massif, which would always appear just out of reach. In the distance, above the darkness of the cable car station, the eye would naturally trace the path of the white pistes coming down from the domed top of the Glacier de Bellecote. The runs came down from the left and the right, with the more gentle gradients directly in front and some impressive black run drop-offs to the left of this mountain.

Emma's brothers were not interested in the view; they had already wrenched their skis out of the external gondola fittings. During the ascent, the skis had seemed to wobble precariously with the moans and groans of the gondola, especially when it passed beneath one of the numerous supporting pylons. This would normally signify a change of direction or gradient and it was clear from the sounds that the gondolas made as they transected these parts of their journey that each of the bubbles were unwilling members of this breathing and living beast, but a beast that enabled so many people to experience the highest mountains in this area of the Alps.

They piled into the next lift car station, sited one hundred metres further on, and again, the three young adults were whooshed onwards and higher, taking them deeper into this fairytale winter wonderland.

The gondolas themselves had limited air circulation and whilst the multitudes of clothing layers were essential once outdoors, being in the gondola meant that within a couple of minutes the occupants were hot, uncomfortable, and the car soon became partially steamed up. Every little bump would pass through them, their heads and entire limbs juddering to the sound of the groaning machine whirring away above them. The cable that was above their heads moved with them, being pulled along and turned round at either of the lifts ends by giant red metallic wheels. A huge generator powered the weight of the lift and this sat in the valley far below.

The gondola swung across the deep valley between the Roche de Mio and the Glacier de Bellecote with the people way down below looking like ants moving along the couple of gentle gradient blue runs. The ants seemed to make slow progress with the speckled colours of their outfits sparkling against the sweep of beautiful white snow. The gondolas all swung into the first lift car station in the valley before then gently rising all the way into the highest lift car station. This top lift car station was positioned at the base of the glacier, perched on a rocky outcrop overlooking valleys on all sides.

The few skiers that had been prepared to take this top lift gondola were starting the process of knocking their boots to remove any excess snow, clipping their boots into their skis and then tightening their boot bindings. As the air was still cool, many were also jumping up and down on the spot or stretching and banging their gloved hands together to improve their circulation.

As soon as all of their kit was in place, they skated across to the chairlift to take them to the beginning of the glacier run down. However, as the group were not going to be skiing back down the glacier, they would take the rickety old two person chair traversing the glacier slope that lay above the main chair, which the lads and Emma were currently hopping onto. What an ordeal, the brothers were thinking, how many chairs and other lifts did they have to catch to experience some quality powder? Neither of her brothers had taken this route before, but Emma knew better. She was well aware that they were all in for a treat and coaxed them on with an excited grin.

CHAPTER 17

The rickety chair juddered, stalled and started protesting at having to heave its occupants across the high Alps and, even with the light breeze at lower altitude on the glacier, the air was biting and crisp and sharp and ate its way through the layers that everyone was wearing.

The young family members did not have to endure the lift's protestations for long. Coming to a bumpy and awkward slow down, the chair continued to carry on whilst the occupants, the two brothers, sat side by side, scrambled out of the first chair. They had forgotten to lift up their metal waist bar, which ensured they were not thrown from the chair whilst in mid-air. Emma much more smoothly pushed off with her back hand away from the front edge of the chair and glided immediately towards the edge of the piste at the very top of the glacier.

Emma's brothers followed her more cautiously over the ridge into the unknown. There was an immediate drop onto a very steep slope, equivalent to at least a forty five degree angle. Despite the near perfect conditions with the sun shining and the light powder snow, it was difficult to see what lay ahead and there were the signs of rocky outcrops, normally indicating cliffs and sheer drops below them.

Emma swung her skis to the right and made a perfect arc, creating fresh tracks in front of her brothers. This was enough for them to want to do similar and invigorated them to put a dazzling collection of closely linked slalom turns together. The party came to a halt above the rocks, which had appeared well below them when they had first jumped off the back of the glacier.

This was a special day and Emma loved every minute. Just her and her brothers, perfect snow and no concerns in her life. Her brothers also seemed pretty contented as they whooped their way down the next few hundred metres of untouched powder.

What happened next happened in a flash and was to change everything.

Sam, the younger brother, clipped an unseen rock with his left ski. He clipped the very edge of the rock at speed, it unbalanced him and he cart-wheeled forward down the steep slope and gained momentum. As is the function of the skis, both of his skis bindings ejected his feet so that his legs were not broken in the tumble.

Emma and her other brother looked in horror as not only did her brother tumble down the slope, but his now separate skis, despite their small brakes which had appeared since the ski boots had been ejected, rapidly continued to gain speed and were thrown over the cliff in front of them. The skis soon plummeted over and there was nothing any of the three of them could do to catch up with them or find them as they flew through the air to the base of the cliffs.

As for her younger brother Sam, he had naturally strung his body weight out to attempt to slow down his falling body. As the rock cliff fast approached he was squealing hysterically, his brother would have said like a girl, but in his mind he was far too young to die and desperate to hang on to anything that presented itself to grab hold of.

Fortunately there were a couple of rocks projecting prior to the cliff face and both his clothing and body snarled against their solidity. There was an agonised shout as Sam became caught up against one of the medium sized jagged rocks positioned close to the edge. Part of the rock had sliced his clothing and become embedded in his lower leg.

Emma and Joseph were not far behind and caught up

within half a minute. The sight at close quarters was not any better than they had expected. Sam's face was drawn and pasty. His skis were nowhere to be seen. There was blood staining his salopettes and his leg was resting at an odd angle. All of the siblings looked at each other in absolute shock and there was a hint of desperation in the air. All was still. It would be two hours before sunset.

CHAPTER 18

Archie had had time to reflect on his team for the mission, and their performances within the target shooting the week before. All of his regular colleagues had succeeded in their training but he was concerned by the attitude demonstrated by one of the potential candidates.

Petty Officer Stuart Betts had reacted badly to failing on the accuracy of his shooting. Archie had detected some noticeable disdain from him since the end of the elimination.

Whenever Archie had tried to talk to Betts, he had avoided eye contact or walked off in the opposite direction.

Archie finished making his cup of tea. He added just a trickle of milk and let the mug rest as he liked his tea strong. He turned and gazed out of his apartment. He had invested in one of the new purpose built flats at Gunwharf Quays close to the Millennium tower on the waterfront of Portsmouth Harbour. The view was impressive, he could see across the waterfront to Gosport and take in all the comings and goings of small craft entering and exiting this narrow stretch of water.

Down below to his left were the historic remnants of what much of Portsmouth would have appeared like prior to the significant bombing in the Second World War. The cobbled narrow streets and overhanging ancient properties sitting on the sandbank making up Portsmouth Hard made it easy to imagine the press-ganging that had occurred hundreds of years before, where unwilling men were signed up to the numerous naval voyages which departed from this historic port.

To his right Archie could see the masts of the old tall ships. The historic *Warrior*, one of the most important and first metal clad warships and the *Victory*, Nelson's Flagship. The most historic of them all, though, lay within a white roofed warehouse. She had been dredged up from the seabed within sight of Southsea Castle with Prince Charles taking a strong interest, and was known as Henry VIII's *Mary Rose*.

Archie could not concentrate on the view. He rarely fell out with people but he believed that this man had not given him a chance. Stuart Betts was definitely one to watch as he was already showing signs of completely erratic behaviour. It had reminded him of his relationship with his brother when he had been growing up.

Brought up in Norfolk, close to the Broads, Archie had always loved water. As a toddler, he was forever told that he had run towards it. Never one to shy away from things, all he had wanted to do was splash around and share his enjoyment by soaking as many other people as possible. This had included his younger brother Ben who was not so keen on water. Ben had let out his howls and screams and inevitably cried when his older sibling took delight at splashing in his direction.

Archie had grown up relishing sailing on those Broads. He would help out and crew one of the dinghies used at Wroxham Broad, enjoying the surroundings with the swans, coots and myriad of ducks always seeming to be in the way of the boats, but never quite being mown down. He had often sailed past the couple of bird islands which humans entered at their own risk.

In the latter stages of primary school, he had pushed his younger brother Ben onto one of the bird islands, having rowed across the few metres from the shore. Sure enough, his four feet tall brother was soon surrounded by geese and swans all trying to peck him off their patch of land. Archie was waiting for the cries of anguish and he was not disappointed. He had set himself up so his brother needed him. The daring rescue of Ben from the bird pecking island was one of a number of family stories that none of the Malcolms would forget.

Archie took a deep swallow from his piping hot, sugarless tea. People thought of him as a fitness fanatic, but he just took care of himself. Perhaps it would do him good to be distracted for at least five minutes. He turned back to the equipment within his flat.

Archie had a couple of scopes so that he could zoom in on the day to day happenings of the Solent. He had always enjoyed the ongoing life of the sea and all of the associations with it.

As he looked through the long telescopic lens he homed in on the hovercraft which had covered most of the distance from Southsea Beach to Ryde on the Isle of Wight. The hovercrafts were an impressive sight. Each of the crafts would literally deflate their air cushion just off the Southsea promenade and the huge fans at their rear would slowly be wound down.

All of this activity could not distract Archie from the issue in his mind. Naval HQ had become aware of coded radio traffic. They did not know what it meant but it involved illegal goods and their overall mission to counter the current ferrying of illegal narcotics into UK borders. His team had been ordered to make an attack against an identified control centre located within the Alps. Archie's superiors had stated that it needed to be quietly put out of action. Quietly seemed to be the important word.

There were too many unanswered questions and Archie's mind raced through them. Who was the perpetrator? What exactly was this control centre? How many people were based there? What were their defences and what would Archie and his team be up against? How would the answers affect Archie's method of attack?

Archie's head began to spin, and he moved the telescope onto a group of three sailing boats which were cruising past the main entrance to Haslar marina.

CHAPTER 19

This year's striking competition was being held at Portsmouth Cathedral. Bands could enter the method ringing section or the call change element or both items. The competition was for the whole of the Winchester & Portsmouth Diocesan Guild, so the standard would be of the highest calibre.

Each band would have two minutes practice. The treble, the highest bell and the first to strike would then ring fully twice at hand-stroke and back-stroke which signified that the five minute test piece was about to be performed.

The judges, who were normally secreted away in a mobile caravan or some sort of temporary shelter, would then mark the faults. If two bells just clipped each other most judges would give this a half fault, but if there was a full on clash or an audible gap which created a pile up among the other bells then the judges would award a full fault. The judges were normally very experienced campanologists who were good at listening.

The bands, who had entered teams to compete, had been practising for the last few months. Striking competitions always brought together many ringers who would otherwise not often see each other and there was a fascinating mood in the air as the village tower groups would eye-up the more advanced Cathedral and large town bands. As usual, there were many who took this type of event incredibly seriously but pretended not to show it.

In this striking competition, no further points were awarded if a more difficult method was chosen and the band made the same amount of mistakes than if they were ringing a more basic method. Therefore, most of the bands would go for a method or call changes that they felt comfortable with.

As bell-ringing is a team activity and totally reliant on the whole band being in the right place, the pressure within the striking competition would be high. The likelihood of anything going wrong, at any moment in time, gave Archie the particular buzz that he was feeling today.

He was very pleased to be able to represent the home Portsmouth Cathedral band, having only been ringing with them for a few years. Furthermore, they were expected to do well. So, yet again, Archie was concentrating hard to push all thoughts of his current mission to the back of his mind and focus on what he enjoyed.

Their practising had gone well with some wonderful striking. This had been a real pleasure to listen to. However, as the occasion had drawn closer, there had been the natural nerves and this had affected a number of the ringers.

As Archie was a younger ringer it was tempting for some of the older lot to blame him, at least partly, for a mistake that a more experienced hand may have made. Whilst Archie understood this mentality, it was something that he was not prepared to accept, if he knew that he was right. In his team player way, Archie was always able to keep everyone on side whilst standing up for himself, and many of the ringers respected him for his attitude.

So it was with excitement and some trepidation that Archie approached the striking contest day and the Portsmouth Cathedral band was on next.

CHAPTER 20

St. Mary's Portsmouth was ringing; a well established and experienced eight bell team. The ringing soon settled into a comfortable rhythm and those that were listening to the ringing picked out the method that was being rung: 'Stedman Triples'.

The heaviest bell and lowest sounding, the tenor, was not involved in moving about within the method and provided a steady dong at the end of each row of ringing. The order of the other bells moved about every stroke and provided the tune to the method.

The strength and quality of the ringing produced by the St. Mary's team did not help the confidence of the Portsmouth Cathedral band who were awaiting their turn. As the ringers, including Archie, gathered at the base of the tower steps, the faces of the individual team members were a picture of nervousness, excitement, concentration and calmness.

At last the sound of the bells above the ringing chamber came to an end. The St. Mary's band filed down the steps and past the ringers waiting to go up. The last member of their team to file past, which was a surprise to Archie and caught him off guard, was David.

Archie had not realised that David would be ringing in this competition, and for the St. Mary's band. Whilst they had rung frequently in the past as teenagers, Archie had completely forgotten that David might be ringing in Portsmouth as well as playing his mixed hockey. When Archie had lived with David in their earlier years as students neither of them had been ringing and it was, after all, with David that he had first been introduced to Emma.

David appeared a little smug as he passed Archie and could not help saying, "Not bad ringing, eh?" Archie could only agree with David. He had been impressed. As he trudged up the tower steps to the ringing chamber he and his fellow ringers had much to live up to.

So they began. The Tower Captain took control and told Mavis on the treble to call the band to order to start the two minutes practice piece. The Portsmouth Cathedral band promptly rang as one; they were sounding good.

The Tower Captain looked at all of his team proudly and just nodded and confirmed, "Good ringing everyone. We just need similar again please and then we'll do as well as anyone."

No response was necessary as the ringers' level of concentration heightened further. Archie could not put David out of his mind. The timing was incredible. Here he was trying to concentrate for his band and somehow the previous ringing by St. Mary's, and the fact that David had been involved, really upset him.

Try as he might to keep his calm, it was one of the few times in his life where Archie was unsettled. The ringing was going well, but Archie could not fully concentrate on keeping his place. Suddenly he was being shouted at sternly and he came to out of his daydream and reddened immediately as he realised that he had just clipped the Tower Captain's bell. Horror! All other thoughts were now out of his mind as he attempted to redeem himself. The ringing soon came to an end and the band stood their bells.

In the presentation later that afternoon all were eagerly awaiting the result of the main striking competition. It was clear that whilst all of the bands had performed well the result would be between St Mary's band and Portsmouth Cathedral.

Both bands had rung to the best of their ability. The judges had been impressed. They then commented on the individual performances, summarising the Stedman Triples rung by the St. Mary's band as "a fine piece of ringing."

Turning to the Portsmouth Cathedral piece, again they commented on an excellently rung method, except for a little clip halfway through. At that moment the whole of the band gazed intently at Archie. The judges decided that, due to this one small mistake, the St. Mary's band would be awarded the striking competition trophy for the current year.

CHAPTER 21

The next boat leaving Lima was a private vessel which had many of the close Morales family aboard.

With the relative fiasco that had occurred delivering the current precious cargo through the Andes to Lima, Natalia and her brothers wanted to ensure that the Morales' family's main trade route to Europe was secure. It was also vital for Natalia to establish the Morales' way with their contacts in the UK and Europe and this needed to be done face to face.

Senor Morales would still oversee the whole operation from his base in Lima. Natalia was his eldest and only daughter, and she had been brought up to look after herself. She knew that she would not let her family down; if she did, there would be trouble. Her life would be at risk.

The Morales family were now settled within their cabins on the freighter *The Islander*, and what they could not know was that two of the tribal men's friends had followed the Morales brothers and the tall Spanish lady with dark, black, shoulder length hair, grey-green eyes and still the dark red lipstick, onto the vessel.

The friends of the tribal men, who had attempted to collect payment and then been dealt with by the Morales brothers, had found their colleagues with broken ribs and broken noses limping back to their humble homes in the mountains. This was not acceptable to any human society and the ways of the Andean tribes meant that the Morales needed to be taught a lesson.

It would be enough for any of the Morales to have an accident. The tribal men did not need to announce themselves. They worked hard on the land. There was no need for them to make a big deal about what they were doing. This was how they lived their everyday lives. Hundreds of years ago they may have let the Spanish think that they had conquered most of South America, but the tribal way of life lived on. The people were too strong emotionally to be conquered and this would be a small token of their resistance.

The Morales brothers reviewed their itinerary, detailing who needed to be seen over the few days that were being spent in the UK. It was a busy schedule and essential that all of the contacts being seen were aware of how the distribution routes needed to be run.

The Morales family could then spend time overseeing the distribution; ensuring that it operated like clockwork. Their sourcing of the supply had highlighted that the Andean routes were clearly becoming at risk and the Bolivian government were currently on the coat-tails of the Morales' existing suppliers. The family were not aware of any issues with their local distribution networks. They appeared strong. It was important that no details could be traced back to them. The many intermediaries were not aware of any information more than one link in the chain away. If they knew anything of the Morales family, then it was because of their impressive international reputation for the quality of their supply of leather goods, rope, hemp and netting.

On the first evening of their fifteen day voyage the Morales were already relaxing in their cabin. The first leg would take them through the Suez Canal and into the Atlantic, prior to their crossing to Portsmouth.

Meanwhile, the two tribal men were having difficulty sleeping. They were cold, tucked away in one of the small life rafts just in front of the bridge. "Pass me some Coca leaves," one of them said. The other looked at him with a slightly glazed expression, grunted, and then tossed over the full bag of dirty green leaves.

CHAPTER 22

Natalia woke in her cabin the following morning and did not want to stir from what had been a fitful night's sleep.

She had been thinking about her life to date and concluded that she had had a difficult route to the present. This was mixed up with the thought that she had pulled herself together and been strong and made a huge success of the chances that she had been given, and this had made her family proud.

Even if her competitors had not respected her techniques for dominating the Lima market in the buying and selling of leatherwear, and the front that the business provided, they did at least admire her for her cunning and hardness.

She had managed to build up her father's business from humble beginnings in a small shop within the centre of Lima. It was when their business branched out that it became successful. Whilst her father had been an excellent negotiator and was always able to command a much higher price for his goods than those that were sold to him from the tribal people, Natalia had taken the business into a whole new realm of success.

With her contacts across South America, Natalia had firmly set up the first major export routes for high value cocaine, with their main market being the UK. The cocaine that arrived in the UK was initially distributed through Portsmouth, and it was from Portsmouth that Natalia ensured that the UK operation was receiving and distributing their valuable supply effectively.

There were risks and, at the beginning, those risks had

been minimal. Many of Natalia's wider family were already involved in the production of the paste in enclaves within the rainforest. The rainforest provided an excellent supply of the raw materials, running water and the ability to hide from the government searches in their helicopters.

Natalia had had the brains to develop the distribution side of the business but needed strong arm help when she met with resistance. In addition there was unacceptable risk from individuals who could not be corrupted and were a hindrance to expansion, or from those who were likely to inform the incorruptible elements of the authorities, where even the Morales family had no power. This was where her brothers played their part.

Whilst they may not have been born with the same intelligence that Natalia possessed, they were athletes and went running every other day. Both brothers were also members of kick-boxing clubs and sparred with each other. Their contacts were of a different nature, as underground Lima ran on threats, violence and the ability to persuade. The brothers and their kick boxing friends and acquaintances soon developed the ability to persuade and it was recognised before very long that you did not want to be on the wrong side of the Morales brothers.

Natalia was still snoozing, and pulled the covers closer to her body, endeavouring to keep the heat from escaping into her large and airy cabin. She dreamed of owning a place in the mountains, a ranch with a masterful husband. He would have to be of strong, Spanish-South American blood. She would have at least a couple of children and land as far as you could see in every direction. This was her dream... she purred and rolled over for some more snoozing. She did not need the beauty sleep. Everyone on the freighter had eyed enough of her beauty. After all, she was the baby sister of the family, the one that should be looked after and taken care of.

CHAPTER 23

The Woodcutter in the discreet wooden chalet in the French Alps had had a swim in the relaxation zone pool above the basement area. He was just having a quick, cool shower before satisfying his enormous appetite. He always looked forward to breakfast. A full fry up was one of his favourite meals and the smell produced whilst he was cooking was enough to take his stomach into full hungry excitement.

He did not stint on the ingredients; sausages, bacon, and a couple of eggs, fried tomato, mushroom and toast. He turned on the radio and continued to improve on his understanding of the fast spoken French that was gushing out of the handset on the kitchen worktop. The weather forecast soon followed and confirmed that the next couple of days were going to be still with clear skies and a freezing level of one thousand six hundred metres before increasing winds and the potential for violent alpine storms and snow showers thereafter. The temperature was also to drop dramatically to the minuses at valley level.

This last news confirmed that it would be necessary to make another supply run and these trips were also enjoyable, though maybe not as satisfying as the full breakfast sizzling away in the pan, wafting itself into every corner of the chalet. Anyway, it was a good excuse to exercise one of the skidoos stored in the basement and take it for a proper outing.

The last of the bacon mopped up the remaining tomato and egg, another perfectly clean plate. No-one could blame him for wasting his food. He picked up his winter clothing, deer stalker hat, and overcoat to go over his fleece and salopette-type trousers. Proceeding to the first floor, he pointed his electronic fob at the door for the second bedroom on the right to ensure that all was secure. A quick glance around confirmed that there was nothing out of place. There were no warning lights or messages requiring a response.

He descended into the basement area and put in the skidoo's emergency locker spare thermals, a torch, rope and first aid kit. Firing up the skidoo and skidding out of the chalet, he used the electronic fob to close up the basement doors. The skidoo's steering was surprisingly stiff and it required some shoulder weight to steer the machine around the side of the property and onto the perfect powder snow.

Once on the snow the skidoo came into its own, cruising across the white powder. The brakes were sensitive. The engine allowed for a top speed of over forty miles an hour, which was an awesome out of control feeling over the wild terrain, but the ride was fairly smooth due to the in-built suspension and make-up of the front skis, which dampened any rough contact. This meant that the rider was able to endure journeys of a couple of hours without feeling too exhausted. The rider did need to ensure that his face and hands were covered, as being in the same position, similar to a motorcycle rider, the cold would eat away at those parts that were exposed or immobile and these areas would become numb.

The black skidoo wound down the valley onto the cross country trails. These trails soon entered the top of the pine forest above the valley floor. They were rutted by the snow plough tracks clearing the essential routes that maintained access to the ski villages above. On skis or a board, these trails give an extremely bumpy ride with pine cones, fallen logs and other hazards but the skidoo absorbed the bumps and troughs and the Woodcutter soon found himself at the local grocery store on the high street of Plagne 1800, below La Plagne. Whilst in the neighbouring valley, it was a different world of civilisation.

No one asked any questions here. He could come and go as he pleased and stock up with whatever he needed. Thirty minutes later he had what he required. Walking swiftly out of the small supermarket, he headed past Chalet Marguerite to the cross country trails. Again, these routes would lead him out into the perfect white and to his wilderness valley.

CHAPTER 24

Once back at the partially hidden chalet, the Woodcutter unloaded his supplies into the store rooms in the basement and bounded up the stairs to the second bedroom on the right. Pointing his electronic fob, the door slid open and he smoothly pushed it aside to start up the computer system. His IT set up allowed the Woodcutter to check on the daily reports that would have been submitted so he could provide the required updates to his controllers.

The previous 'Code White' situation had seriously alarmed all in the operation. It was not clear how it had happened but it was likely that there was a leak, and all leaks needed to be permanently stemmed.

The computer buzzed to life. He went through the current deliveries to confirm that they were all on track. From his remote cabin he had access to the Earth's many satellites and using his global positioning system against those that were transmitting from each of the deliveries, there was an instant view of the state of play of the operation.

It would have been too dangerous for his controllers to have had this information to hand in the UK, as the authorities would have been sure to have tracked down the unusual signals and amount of power being used.

In the high Alps, the remoteness of the chalet in its pristine wilderness meant that this valley had been overlooked so far.

Going through the deliveries, all of the stock from the *Alana Princess* was now where it should be in the pipeline. The cargo had been unloaded successfully and the handlers were at the processing stage. His contacts required payment, but this was just a matter of time.

The *Juliano*, which had temporarily docked in Plymouth since the news of the Code White, was now on her way to Portsmouth and would be unloading within the next forty eight hours. She would require special attention since the close call with the *Alana Princess*, and to ensure that she was unloading just like any other fishing vessel.

As Portsmouth no longer had a regular fishing fleet, the whole operation had had to set up their own new fishing terminal. It had gone down well with the locals, who were not used to fresh sea produce. Much of the fish supplied the local restaurants on the seafront in Southsea and Old Portsmouth. The other element of the stock was carefully distributed across the UK in the usual method and the local points of contact were responsible for its successful onward transportation.

Scrolling through the current reports, the Woodcutter noticed that the main South American distributor had recently left Lima on board the scheduled freighter and would be arriving in Portsmouth in less than two weeks. He was aware of their reputation and it was of no concern to him. He had experienced his fair share of run-ins with the law, with ex-colleagues and these type of people. His military past was behind him now, but if he had to use some of his past training, he would. It had helped him on many occasions to stay alive and he was not planning on leaving this Earth anytime soon.

He had been given his specialist work to do, and he performed it well. His overseeing of the state of play of the operation provided the valuable information to the main distributor so that they could feed this knowledge onto the supply chain. This network of providers would then know the quantities required. The Woodcutter would similarly check on the progress of the off-loading of the stock and onward distribution.

He reflected on the importance of his work feeding information back to his overall controllers. He shifted in his seat and his eye twitched, for as well as making a living, he felt bitter now; his young wife and teenage daughter's lives depended on it.

CHAPTER 25

Petty Officer Stuart Betts's behaviour had completely changed. He was being a model naval Non-Commissioned Officer and doing everything Lieutenant Archie Malcolm and Commander Edgar Bennett required for the mission to go ahead as planned.

Furthermore, Petty Officer Betts had been on the shooting practice range whenever time allowed, and was boosting team camaraderie at every opportunity. Archie had had a change of heart and thought he would be a valuable member of the team. With his vast practical experience, (he had served for over twenty years,) he would be useful if they were up against it.

Lieutenant Malcolm decided that in leading the team, with Petty Officer Betts providing some experience, he would also need several of his reliable core group. These were crack marksmen in peak physical condition, with whom he had served for a number of years, and they weren't all men.

Jackie and Jo were as tough as any of them, in excellent physical shape and perfect shots. In addition to Jackie and Jo, were Nick, Kevin and James. The seven of them had to work as a close unit. Kevin would handle the communications and Nick and James were experienced in Arctic and Alpine conditions and would scout the ground that lay ahead.

As Archie walked across to the map table there were reconnaissance pictures strewn across the whole of the glass top. Jackie and Jo had been going through the layout of the Alpine area that the team were to be in, searching for signs of installations that could be a threat to them when on the ground.

Commander Edgar Bennett appeared and loomed over Lieutenant Malcolm's shoulder. He started to point at the map table and confirmed what the team already knew:

"The coded radio traffic was believed to be emitted from this valley close to the resort town of La Plagne in the French Alps. There is a scheduled air drop at 08:00 hrs with your team to depart at 06:00. Do not be late and ensure that you come back with further information as to what is going on. You may use whatever force is necessary to ascertain what threat is being imposed on the United Kingdom and please do remember this operation is to be strictly between these four walls, is that all understood?"

The entire team answered as one: "Yes, sir."

So they were on for the following morning. This was it. Archie's moment of glory or failure. The mission was his responsibility and he would be making the decisions on the ground that would be affecting the lives of his six team members. He was unlikely to sleep, but he then remembered it was practice night at the Cathedral.

He had let the ringing team down in the recent striking competition. All had told him that it was not his fault but it still hurt. To have come a close second to St Mary's was not good news. They were the chief rivals and David had been in their band. It was not like Archie to mull over this issue. He needed to pull himself together.

Archie de-briefed the team and left them until 05:30 when they would be meeting prior to their departure at 06:00. He collected his cap and coat and, as usual, rushed out past Monica, who he blew a kiss at, just to gain a reaction. He was not disappointed by the scowl of the response, but he was sure that she had given a small, sly wink just before he swiped his card to let himself out and he walked hurriedly past the sentries at the main gate.

Archie walked up the spiral staircase and greeted the

Tower Captain and Mavis who were already in the ringing chamber. The rest of the band arrived within the next few minutes and the Tower Captain made a point of saying to everyone:

"We *all* did fantastically in the striking competition and we are pleased that Portsmouth Cathedral achieved as much as we did. It is important for us to go forward from what we have achieved and look to bring the trophy back next year."

There was an air of calm. Everyone in the room agreed. There were nods and a "Here, here." Then the Tower Captain called everyone to order, "Now for some ringing. Yorkshire Royal please. Archie you are involved."

The ringing sounded wonderful. All were inspired and Archie felt cleansed, being able to move forward again with his head held high.

CHAPTER 26

The ringing the night before had helped Archie to sleep. His bright blue, old-fashioned alarm clock with a large face and proper hands had reverberated within his tiny flat.

He had to slam his hand down on the top of the clock between the two silver bells to stop the whirring so that it just continued to tick tock, tick tock...

The darkness did not help to coax him into rising from his bed. It was only in the hot shower that his eyes and head and body came to life. Now was the time to prove himself, for he had been given quite an opportunity.

It was as a teenager that he had originally proven himself. Archie had branched out into team sports. Being a natural sportsman, he ended up representing his Norfolk area, as well as his school, for hockey and cricket. He loved the games, yet never boasted or took sides. In doing so, his peers, both friends and those that knew him only vaguely, respected him and he was one of the handful at school who you knew would listen to their colleagues. He had rare non-judgemental qualities and was a natural team player, always striving to better the position of the group. It was this mental attitude and in-built sports skill which saw Archie lead the hockey firsts through to regional victory in the schools championship, in his last year at school. As Vice Captain of the cricket team he had battled to ensure their position as runners up in their regional league.

Once at university he had been sponsored to train within specialist areas of the Navy and to continue his studies of oceanography. The hot water of the shower brought Archie back to the present, the steam condensing against the small bathroom mirror.

Once out of the shower, he threw on his non-descript clothes and webbing, grabbed his pack and jogged round to the naval base. The whole team squeezed into the back of the pale blue transit van. None of the group had been told of their departure point for security reasons. It would be taken care of. Commander Edgar Bennett would ensure there was a smooth start to their mission.

Since their initial training back in early autumn, all of his team had come a long way. It was now well into the ski season and the team were aware of the significant quantities of snow on the ground. Many of the group had honed their board riding and skiing at the ski slopes nearby. This had been combined with regular training sessions at the Naval gym and in the Naval sports complexes in Portsmouth.

As each of the group boarded the light plane to take them to the identified drop zone, Archie checked their equipment was in place and that each member of his team had collated all that was required for Stage 1: Departure, Flight and Drop.

All was present and correct. Jackie and Jo had copies of all the reconnaissance memorised in their heads as it would not do to be found with any details of this mission on them. None of them bore any markings on their clothing of any particular country, or carried any items that could be specifically traced back to the UK. James and Nick had their specialist marksmen rifles and telescopes in order that they could scout ahead. Kevin had some impressive satellite communications equipment strapped inside his arctic warfare rucksack. Archie had standard kit but also carried a hunting knife he had always used and a flare to help bring them all home. Stuart Betts sat just behind Archie, contemplating the next few hours, at least this was the impression that he gave, staring into the hold of the small plane.

The propellers of the plane whirred into action. The body rocked forward off its blocks and proceeded to transit to the runway and into the darkness. The darkness was starting to give way to an eerie early morning light, it still not being dawn.

The plane only needed a short runway and this airport was ideal. It was not normally used and lay tucked away from Portsea Island. Few were aware of any aircraft ever taking off or landing at this site. The location was extremely discreet and allowed the takeoff to be completed without notice or comment.

It was cold on board the plane but the occupants were wrapped up warm in their winter survival clothing. They each had a parachute attached to their backs and were carrying out the standard checks with each other to ensure that all would go according to plan.

Buffeted by the increasing wind, the plane started to creak and whisper and howl whilst all else was quiet. The weather forecast indicated calm conditions over the next twenty four hours before storm conditions coming in from the north. However, it appeared that the storm was coming on apace and this was not ideal. The team would have to work extremely quickly.

The pilot nodded confirmation to Archie and raised his right hand to indicate thirty minutes until the drop zone, which was immediately relayed to the whole team. Archie was now full of adrenalin and raring to go.

All of the planning and organisation had led up to this point. His team was aware of their rendezvous at the head of the valley, a location which provided slight cover below the Glacier de Bellecote. They would then ski over to the target valley and go into surveillance mode to gather as much information as possible before further movement and decision making.

The plane hatch was opened and the cool air gushed in like a small rocket igniting. James and Nick, as scouts, shuffled over to the opening and awaited Archie's signal. It was difficult for them to see anything below in the dawn. Archie also waited as he was reliant on the signal from the pilot.

At last the pilot held his hand up and made a clear thumbs up sign to Archie. Archie clapped his left hand on Nick's shoulder. Nick did not need to be patted twice. Off through the hatch and into the freezing cold air the two men jumped, quickly replaced at the hatch by Kevin and then Jackie and Jo, Stuart Betts and lastly Archie. The pilot provided the OK and V signals for best of British luck and Archie returned the gestures before plummeting out of the aircraft and to the ground below.

CHAPTER 27

Emma and her brothers were stone cold.

She and her elder brother Joseph had managed to keep Sam with them, although he was slipping in and out of consciousness. His leg had been knocked out of its normal position and, whilst not medically trained, Emma and Joseph were sure that it was broken. The fact that it was lying at an odd angle when they had caught up with Sam meant that they had come to this conclusion within the first minute of looking at their younger brother.

With only two hours prior to sunset, they had agonised as to what to do. There was no way that it would be possible to move Sam to anywhere habitable before nightfall. They had taken the difficult decision of finding somewhere as close as possible with shelter, for them all to make it through the night. Emma or Joseph would set off for help with the light of the dawn.

Fortunately, Emma had had an orange survival bag in her rucksack and an extra warm top. They had no other provisions. Joseph had tied one of Sam's ski poles to his painful leg to fashion a makeshift splint. He had used the cord from his sunglasses to keep them from falling off. The splint meant that Sam would keep his leg straight and not intentionally cause himself any further harm.

The siblings had jiggled themselves into the survival bag still close to the rocks and were wearing every item of warm clothing that each of them had brought out with them. Joseph, Emma and Sam all had gloves and hats, full salopettes covering their legs and ski jackets. Underneath the ski jackets they each just had a fleece and a base layer. Whilst relatively warm together, the sun was now low in the sky and being near the top of the glacier the temperature was soon to plunge.

The bright orange of the survival bag would be seen from hundreds of metres away but they would not be reported missing until well after dark. Their parents knew they were all together and would expect them to have a *gluwein* or mulled wine in Plagne Centre prior to returning to the chalet. Emma and Joseph and Sam would not be missed until the chalet evening meal at eight o'clock. Even then, their parents thought that their children were to be skiing on all of the marked pistes within the region, and certainly not venturing off the back of the Glacier de Bellecote. It would be some search party that would find them where they were presently located.

Emma felt the breeze on her exposed cheek. The wind was seriously picking up and she was losing body warmth, fast. This was just what they needed! It had been relatively still and calm until an hour ago and now the weather was rapidly changing. She tried to cuddle up to her brothers but there was no real warmth being emitted from them. She kept curling her gloved hands into fists and was starting to shiver uncontrollably, even though she was within the orange survival bag. Joseph felt Emma struggling to stay warm and he too was cold, colder than he had been for years. Emma was attempting to think of her student life back in Portsmouth against the current circumstances that she was in.

Emma studied geography and lived in an all-girl student house on Kent Road in Southsea. She had been in a hall of residence in her first year and had originally made friends with the other girls on her course.

Given that the Isle of Portsmouth is only approximately four miles long and three miles wide, she had been able to be near to her main campus. Her geography building, the library and the Student Union were all situated in the north west of Southsea. Yet Emma also wanted to be as close as possible to the beach and the fun of the waterfront. This left only a few streets for her and her friends to focus on. Their search had concentrated on the roads to the south of Southsea, close to the Common, the seafront and her campus buildings.

They had settled for an imposing three-storey, turn of the twentieth century, terrace property with grand, high ceilings and large rooms. Whilst the communal area was small and the kitchen area a little shabby and run down, the house afforded quick access to the pebbly beach. By walking five minutes across Southsea Common, she could walk along the ramparts of Old Portsmouth around to the Harbour Entrance or wander in the other direction to Southsea Shopping Centre. It did not have all the shopping stores that she had been used to growing up in Wimbledon, South West London, but it had everything that she needed and that was all that mattered to her.

The location had helped Emma to become extremely fit over the last year, cycling to lectures, running along the three mile waterfront and playing hockey for Portsmouth University.

Joseph, meanwhile, was remaining strong for his sister Emma but even more so for his brother Sam, his closest friend. Joseph had started his first year at university and been accepted by Downing College, Cambridge to read English. It had been the first few months that he had ever been away from his twin brother. He had missed the daily banter and joking that he could have with Sam, and had been looking forward to this family ski holiday for the last couple of months.

Sam had decided to stay on, living at their parents' house in Wimbledon, and pursue a gap year. He had been working hard in many temporary jobs to build up the finances to travel later on in the year, prior to going to university through deferred entry.

Joseph shouted at Sam to wake up. This stirred Emma too. He started humming one of the James Bond theme tunes that they both enjoyed, especially when whizzing down the slopes at high speed. Emma joined in and, at last, a whisper of a hum came from Sam.

Each of them was reflecting that all three of them were together. Still in one piece, well Sam was almost in a couple of pieces, but just about alive and, whilst there was no chance of sleep through the night, Emma, Sam and Joseph would keep each other going until the morning.

Emma had fallen into semi-consciousness by the early dawn so it was Joseph who heard the rasping wind being gently broken by the soft but audible hum of the light plane above. It sounded like a remote control car in his dream but no, this was real and becoming louder. He elbowed Sam, who groaned, and shook Emma awake.

It took a couple of minutes for her to realise what the noise was, why she had been woken up, where she was and why the noise was so important for them.

CHAPTER 28

As he descended into the unknown, Archie Malcolm loved the momentary floating feeling with the air flying up past him, pushing his head up and putting pressure against every part of his body. It always seemed to batter his forehead and buffet his face and nose and mouth. An exhilarating experience.

These feelings were second only to pulling the parachute cord and feeling, or not feeling, the deceleration. The Earth went from visibly rising up to meet Archie as fast as gravity would allow, to a sudden sensation of calm.

He could now take in what was below him and he frowned, for this was wrong and not anywhere near the landing site that had been planned.

The wind had picked up and must have thrown the team off course, he pondered… but the pilot should have taken the strength of the wind into his calculations. The snow covered ground and the castellated ridge adjoining a… glacier? It was becoming slightly clearer in this difficult half-light and now Archie was concerned.

The only glacier in this immediate area was the Glacier de Bellecote and his team were supposed to be landing well below this mountain with the cover that it provided. Too late now. It appeared that Archie and the rest of his team were going to be scattered on much higher perches.

Archie braced himself for the impact of landing. He had chosen what appeared to be a high ledge. It seemed relatively flat from the view that he had, just over the lip of the main glacier. He picked up his legs to cushion the ground that was coming up at him more quickly than usual, and the wind was determined to side swipe him off his planned landing area. Well, the wind would not win and he was going to do everything as per the textbook.

Archie's perfect landing allowed him to have a quick look about him prior to touch down. Whilst he had lost sight of Petty Officer Stuart Bett's parachute, he had homed in on Jackie and Jo's landing site which was fifty metres above him. He stowed all of his parachute material within the next five minutes. He then scrambled upwards from the ledge against the biting wind in thick powder, with skis strapped to the back of his rucksack. Archie then reported his position on his CB radio and five minutes later Jackie and Jo appeared from just above where he was standing.

The girls reported that they had seen the scouts' parachutes land slightly further down the mountain. Worryingly, they had lost the path of Kevin who had jumped immediately before them, and Stuart who had been just behind them, prior to opening his parachute.

Archie reported his position for a second time and he picked up the mumbled responses from Nick and James. All was still quiet from Betts and Kevin. Archie and the girls proceeded to fasten on their skis and head further down the powdered side of the mountain.

In the distance, there was a flash of orange, partially covered in snow, and the three naval service personnel went to investigate.

CHAPTER 29

Archie strode purposefully towards the glint of orange that he thought he had seen from the snow ledge only moments earlier.

Jo and Jackie raced to keep up, their kit appearing to dwarf their smaller frames. Why would there be any unnatural colours in this wilderness? It was important that nothing from their mission had gone astray. Archie was confident that the orange material had nothing to do with Betts or Kevin, for there had been no orange equipment as part of their apparel.

As he approached closer he could make out that it was a winter survival bag and two heads were clearly visible. As he moved forward to within twenty metres he noticed the jagged rocks and the cliff edge.

These people could compromise his mission, he had specific timetables and information that needed to be sourced. He had to ignore whatever position they were in and let the elements take their course. With the light starting to come up, they should be found by a rescue team during the day, if they had been reported missing.

Archie turned away and went back to Jackie and Jo. As he did so, one of the previous two faces that had been within the survival bag had managed to stumble to his feet and was trying to shout "Help, help," but it came out as a raspy, low voiced call. Still, it was enough to catch the attention of the three specialist troops who were hurriedly discussing their best course of action.

Archie had decided that he would inform the authorities over his high powered radio and leave the scene with his team as quickly as they could. The young lad now stumbling over to him had other ideas. He was still calling "Help, help" but now his tone was more desperate and frantic. Archie could not stop himself and went to see what the position was with the young lad and whoever else was in the orange survival bag.

It was one of those ridiculous coincidences that you never want to happen. You go on holiday to a faraway destination to have some peace and quiet and you find that your neighbours, the loud family next door, have booked into the apartment adjacent to yours for the whole week. As Archie peered into the orange survival bag and took in the shape of the other young lad with the makeshift splint put together out of a ski pole and some cord, he also absorbed the figure, seemingly also dazed and partially conscious, of Emma.

Yes, it was clear that it was Emma, although he had just stopped and stared for possibly the last half a minute, waiting for his breathing to turn to near normal and to allow his brain to catch up and think clearly.

Archie was not a swearing man but what the f*** was Emma doing out here in a survival bag, barely conscious, with these two other young lads?

He was confident that both the young lad and Emma in the survival bag would never be aware of any visitors to their picturesque stop but this other lad who had just stumbled in the thick powder snow at Archie's feet could cause trouble.

Archie radioed the French authorities and gave them the coordinates, as best he was able, to where they currently stood. He asked for an estimated time of arrival to which he was told one hour. Good, more than enough time for his whole team to be out of the area and back on track with their mission.

He then went back to the survival bag and made sure that each of the occupants had enough water and provided some snack bars and a further warm survival blanket from his pack and told the young lad who was now being pushed back into the survival bag by Jackie and Jo to wrap up his companions and himself with this further survival blanket.

With the snackbars, water and the start of a new day, the young adults would last for another hour until the French rescue teams saved them from their plight.

CHAPTER 30

David returned from the striking competition feeling great. He had not known that Archie was now ringing for the Portsmouth Cathedral band.

Whilst having invited Archie to his recent birthday party on the River Wye, David had not managed to talk to Archie and catch up. If he remembered rightly, Archie had had to leave in a hurry for some urgent issue. Well, in his view, that had just been rude.

David thought back to his birthday. It had gone well. The time spent Canadian canoeing on the River Wye had meant that he could spend more quality time with many of his friends, and that included the special time spent with Emma. David had grabbed the sleekest looking Canadian canoe and insisted that Emma sit in the front. David took the helm and enjoyed the view downstream, which then just happened to include Emma. Emma and David laughed and joked and struck up good conversation, even if David did like to talk about himself.

Originally, their friendship had started playing mixed hockey and this had developed over the last full year, during their time as students. It was only recently that Archie had met Emma and that had been a shame, David thought.

David was a natural sportsman. He had been at secondary school with Archie in East Anglia and they had both decided to go onto Portsmouth University. Whilst Archie had read oceanography, David had always been interested in how things worked, how they were made up and therefore he naturally fell for engineering. He had gone straight into a hall of residence on the seafront and joined all of the sports teams that he could. Competitive and with a will to win, he continued to excel at hockey but also played football and was a strong swimmer, competing for Portsmouth in the water polo team.

Surprisingly, David had had a difficult past and he kept this under wraps. There were very few people, apart from Archie and a couple of his previous teachers, who knew that David was brought up in a foster home. Both of his parents had died in a small plane crash when he was three years old. They had been on a romantic flight to see their local area from above. The grandparents caring for David whilst his parents flew above had passed away soon after and there were no other surviving relatives. Social Services had taken over David's life.

Passed from home to home, David had suffered. He had found it difficult to confide in adults after earlier bad experiences. Ignored or, even worse, pulled to one side by a specialist counsellor, David just wanted to be allowed to be part of real society, to be free of his bonds, to do what he wanted to do.

There had been a number of other children prepared to play football and David naturally showed enough flair and ability to always be picked by the team leaders. In his young teens, he progressed to usually being one of the team captains. He would drive his team members on until his side won, or slump his shoulders in disgust if they had performed poorly.

He was bright, and despite being passed from home to home with different adults to care for him, David was naturally able. He was awarded a scholarship at the East Anglian secondary school and David was one of the minority of boarders who lived in dormitories at the school. At the beginning, the school saved him. With the opportunity to involve himself in all the sports available, football, hockey, swimming and athletics and enjoy maths, physics and chemistry, David went from strength to strength.

When David was in the sixth form he was allowed to walk into the town centre at lunchtime. He would catch up with the latest album and single releases in the music stores, walk along the river and stroll around the main market square.

It was in the market square that David and a couple of other fellow borders would have a quick smoke, out of the sight of any of the teachers or any other students.

It was also in the market square that he was offered his first real smoke. He was unsure of what he was being offered. David took the roll up and passed over much of his daily allowance. Unfortunately, he also never looked back. Starting with cannabis, David progressed to pills and harder drugs but he was skilled at disguising his hobby. He was sure that Archie did not know and Emma would never find out.

CHAPTER 31

David still lived in his hall of residence, away from Emma and Archie, based in the centre of Portsmouth near to the Guildhall.

There were a couple of hundred students there, and it served their purposes well. Located close to the central shopping district and within walking distance of all the student facilities, the lecture theatres, library, student union and nightlife meant that everything was in close proximity for the students to live a full life within the very centre of the city.

This was important as most students did not have a car. There was a strong contingent of cyclists but the majority used the buses if they needed to, or, to try and keep in check their student debt, they walked everywhere it was practically possible.

David did not have a car and this had helped him to become familiar with the town centre. Portsmouth's core had a small and dense layout, with few landscaped areas. The main green, open space was Southsea Common, which extended to the seafront itself. The only park in the city centre, comprising a small aviary and plant house, was no substitute for the East Anglian fens where David had grown up.

David regularly walked through this central park on his way to or from his engineering block. He would stop and stare at the beautiful birds caught up within their large cages. The birds were quite a sight but many of the larger, colourful specimens were separated so that they were totally on their own. David thought to himself that he often felt how these birds must; trapped in their own surroundings and unable to fly away.

He had to get away from it all, he just needed to meet the right person and then they could move to another part of the country, start afresh, anew, put the past behind them. David would then be away from other activities that had distracted him over the last couple of years, which had embedded him in a tangled web of deceit and lies.

Money was an issue. The scholarship place had been funded by the school and allowed him to come to Portsmouth University to study engineering but David had no funds of his own.

He was now seriously in debt and all of the temporary student jobs in the cafes and bars really did not attract him. The timing of the work always required a shift in the evening when David took part in his sporting activities or went bell-ringing. Other work, such as helping out in the library or turning up to be part of identification parades at the local police station, did not last long and again did not pay very well.

David was aware that he could obtain cocaine very cheaply, as Portsmouth seemed to be a major route into the UK for the drug, and sell it onto a network of contacts both within his hall of residence and throughout the wider Portsmouth city centre community. This would pay him extremely well for minimal work and as long as he kept his head down from the authorities, he would pay his debts off in no time. This was the direction that David chose.

CHAPTER 32

The freighter pulled slowly away from the Suez Canal, easing itself into the Atlantic Ocean. Natalia and her brothers had finished a light salad lunch and were playing cards together in the lounge, just a couple of metres behind the bridge.

The Captain was on watch and loved Cuban Havana cigars. He was a larger than life character with a blue cravat tied loosely around his wide neck. He wore brown chinos and a strong leather belt to ensure that his trousers stayed up around his ample girth. His feet were covered with strong walking boots to ensure that he had a trusted grip on all of the decks and he was excited by his forthcoming retirement.

Captain 'Sharkey' was so called because he had survived a shark attack. An extremely rare incident, he had the remains of the wounds to the side of his stomach to prove it, albeit it had happened over twenty years ago.

There was only a crew of seven for the boat and they all heralded from Lima. Brought up within the city, the sailors had sought to travel the world. A surprising amount of time was spent on the freighters, with weekends off being unheard of. Their ships would only be based at ports to load and dock containers for twelve or twenty four hours. Therefore the crew's lives were spent onboard, experiencing the monotony of keeping the ship going and relaxing by playing cards, reading and the structure of the watches.

It was on the following night after leaving the Suez Canal that the two tribal stowaways put their plan into action.

It had been the Morales brothers who had inflicted the damage on their friends. The Morales' Spanish lady did not bother them so much. Whilst she represented a family who were resented by many of the tribal peoples, she had provided a number of the Andean villages with a selling outlet for their wares. What the tribal villagers were angry about was how the brothers had taught their own village people a physically violent lesson. The fact that much of the delivery had not reached the Morales had been out of their control.

In the early hours of the following morning, the tribesmen lured the brothers out of their cabin by pouring diesel under the door and setting fire to it. The Morales brothers, dazed and confused from being woken mid-sleep, attempted to run down the corridor outside their cabin.

The diesel had set light to the wooden door frame extremely quickly and heavy smoke was billowing along the passageway. There were few lights on outside the cabin and the brothers were unsteady on their feet.

The tribal men had located themselves further down this outside gangway and, in the middle of the night, the freighter's exterior railing led to a dark abyss beyond. There was the hum of the freighter's generators and the swishing sound of the ocean below. All else was quiet.

As the brothers attempted to raise the alarm by shouting that their cabin was on fire, the tribal villagers approached the two men from their rear. As if they were preparing a goat for a feast, the men muffled the cries of the Morales brothers with one hand and slit their throats with the other.

Helping each other to lift the bodies – they were still warm and twitching – the tribesmen heaved with all their strength to move them to the railing of the freighter and then pushed them over the side. There was no remorse and they hugged each other after the bodies had slipped away into the waiting waves below.

Time had been spent over the sleepless, cold days and nights preparing their life-raft, located on the other side of the ship for departure. The fire alarm rang out at last and lights started to cascade the ship in an eerie glow as the tribesmen rapidly took the cover off the smaller boat, ensured that the stolen provisions and Global Positioning System was on board, and started to operate the electronic crane.

As expected, as the bridge realised that the fire alarm was sounding across the ship, the night watchman on shift lowered the power to the turbines. The freighter would take another mile to slow down to walking pace. The tribesmen were ready to take advantage of the slowly moving freighter. The life-raft would be brought to bear on the water so that it was facing in the same direction as the freighter and adjoining the mother ship. They would then sail away, back to the South American coastline.

Unfortunately for the tribal stowaways, Captain Sharkey had quickly toured as much of the outer walkway as practically possible. He noticed that the life-raft was being removed and grappled with the weathered controls to stop it leaving his ship. One of the vertical ropes managed to snag itself in the crane mechanism so that the life-raft lurched forward. The tribal men were holding on for their lives as neither of them could swim. They were manically seeking to cut through the crane ropes and release themselves from the ties that kept the small vessel dangling beside the freighter. Ultimately, the life-raft tipped up as the bow rope split and the stern rope took the entire weight of the boat. The craft dangled vertically downward and the tribesmen were catapulted into the Atlantic, swallowed by the dark seas. The crests of the waves glowed, lit by the fire burning on the freighter.

CHAPTER 33

The sound of the fire alarm stirred Natalia, who was sleeping in a neighbouring cabin to her brothers. What had caused it to go off at this time of the night? Probably a fault in the system or a clumsy oaf knocking one of the fire alarm break glass buttons, she thought from the comfort of her bed.

Then the Captain was knocking on her door. "Get up, get up!" he was shouting. "This is not a drill, everyone to the foredeck!"

The foredeck was located at the front of the ship, just behind the bow. The bridge looked out over the foredeck, much of which was covered in freight containers. There was a central vacant area that also held life vests and there was a fire alarm gathering point in the event of a real alarm sounding.

The Captain and seven crew had quickly ensured their few passengers, including Natalia, were safe after the alarm had been set off.

Natalia hurried to put on her dressing gown and grabbed a warm coat and sensible shoes. She slammed the door of her cabin, and the Captain seemed to sigh and grab her at the same time, forcing her to shuffle as fast as she was able, whilst still in semi-sleep, along the exterior walkway outside of her cabin and to the foredeck. She could smell burning and could not help herself from turning her head around to see where it was coming from.

The passageway was lit up further down the deck. The cabins next to Natalia's were engulfed in flames that were licking and curling around the edges of their doors. A four man team of the seven man crew had found fire extinguishers and a hose. They were doing their best to stop the flames from spreading any further, although they had not managed to enter the rooms where the fire was raging and acting as a furnace.

Natalia fully woke up with a start. Where were her brothers? Had they stayed playing cards into the early hours of the morning in the games room located behind the bridge? Or had they returned to their cabins? She had to find out as she had just witnessed their cabin engulfed in flame and smoke.

She looked at the Captain and started to ask the question. Her eyes were huge and started to fill with tears. The Captain hugged her and said that he had to see to his men and put the fire out. Otherwise they were all in danger and might have to abandon the ship.

Natalia was frantic. The misty glow of the lights that were pouring off the freighter outlined her shadow. She was determined to hold it together. She was strong. She was going to keep the business running and growing. This consignment was to reach the UK safe and well and make the Morales family a huge amount of money. She was to ensure that the supply routes and distribution network were as the family would want, and nothing would stop her from that.

CHAPTER 34

Whilst thinking about his young wife and teenage daughter, he had allowed himself a picture of them together by his main computer in his den of electronics, both the Woodcutter's pager and his computer flashed their warning lights.

For both his computer and pager to be showing their alarm signals was extremely concerning and had not happened before. Before examining the information available to him, he concluded that there had to be a breakdown of security and if so, the whole operation was threatened.

Inputting the specific passwords to see exactly what the detail confirmed to him, he was quickly aware that the main freighter consignment currently crossing the Atlantic had slowed down and there was a fire on board. There was no further information.

The whole operation was potentially in jeopardy. He stared hard at the photograph of his family. It did not bear thinking of what might happen to his wife and soon to be grown up child, if the distribution of the precious cargo of *The Islander* did not go according to plan. This boat was the big one, and was destined to make them all their fortunes. It was his duty to report the position to his controllers and see what action they desired to take.

Having been overseeing the comings and goings of the different supply ships for a number of months, the Woodcutter was nervous. There had been no issues until the *Alana Princess* check, and now the main freighter was under threat. He did not believe in coincidences or unexpected surprises, and nor did his bosses.

It, therefore, was not a surprise when the Woodcutter received a coded response seven minutes after he had provided his warning update to his controllers. It was what he had dreaded. The signal came through as Code Red.

He again thought of his family. What would happen to them? He thought about his last few months in this gilded cage of a paradise. He had always loved the Alps and was a winter sports enthusiast. During his time in the military, he had had regular training in Norway and was an adept skier and survival expert. He had had more than enough time on his own, examining his position and it had allowed him to think about what was important to him.

He stared at the picture again, and traced the outline of the figures with his forefinger.

He had forty-eight hours to make his preparations. After that, he would not be at the pristine chalet in the beautiful wilderness valley or have use of the relaxation zone, the skidoos based in the basement below or the climbing equipment. He had to clear out, lie low and potentially set up anew. The message was very clear.

CHAPTER 35

Petty Officer Stuart Betts lived a surprisingly comfortable lifestyle. He had only recently found himself able to afford some of life's luxuries that he had dreamt about over a long, hard career.

When he had first started in the Navy with the enthusiasm and passionate ambition of youth, the young Able Seaman Betts was desperate to see the world and prove himself. It was a time when he had not been bothered about material goods or wealth.

Since rising to the Non-Commissioned Officer rank of Petty Officer he knew that he was not going to advance any further. Betts was on the edge of retirement and wanted to go out with a bang. Whilst the military pension would pay adequately, and was one of the key perks of the role, it would never make him rich or allow him to pursue some of the interests that he wanted to be involved in, once retired.

His hair had started to grey, activities were slightly more difficult, and he still could not believe that he had been millimetres out on the target shooting selection for Lieutenant Archie Malcolm's secret mission.

Serious work had been required to be back on side with the Lieutenant. It had been extremely difficult to hide his true feelings from both Lieutenant Malcolm and Commander Edgar Bennett, and it had taken skillful repair work to ensure that he was offered a place on the mission.

If he was to achieve his dream of being comfortable in retirement, well, he chuckled quietly to himself, much more than comfortable, then he needed to carry out his objectives to the letter, and as quickly as possible, without being caught.

At last, he felt alive and challenged again, and he had a purpose in life. He continued to stare at the aircraft ceiling; the monotony of the flight at this half-light morning hour meant that his body clock was objecting to the early morning start.

He willed himself to snap awake. This was his opportunity to show just who the most skilled soldier was in this little contingent. He had proven life skills and was highly experienced. He would show his handlers just how experienced he was. They would then honour his own mission contract by transferring further monies to his bank account.

The Petty Officer was next to jump. The Lieutenant had just dropped out of the hatch and Betts was the last of the group to go. He had noticed that James and Nick had exited at almost the same time, as had Jackie and Jo. Kevin, who had left just before the girls, had been weighed down by his communications equipment and had had to shuffle across to the aircraft's hatch opening. It was Kevin's chute he would follow.

As Stuart Betts was freefalling, and enjoying all of the wonderful sensations that are associated with it, he took in Lieutenant Malcolm's parachute direction across to the side of the glacier where he could see Jackie and Jo's chutes lower down. Despite the half-light, Betts thanked whoever had gifted him with such good vision. For as long as he could remember his 20:20 eyesight had served him remarkably well. One of the reasons that he was such an excellent shot was due to his perfect eyesight.

The Petty Officer let himself freefall for a few seconds longer so that he could catch up with Kevin, who was bearing to the wrong side of the glacier. Perfect, this would serve him well, Betts thought.

It had taken surprisingly little money to convince the pilot to drop them off at slightly revised coordinates, the Pilot had half believed it was a last minute change to the plan. However, in order for him not to mention the revised drop off location to anyone else in the party, Betts had passed him a number of notes more and the Pilot just carried out his part of the drop off without reaction.

Kevin's landing was clumsy due to the weight of his kit. He had lost sight of the parachutes of the rest of the team halfway down his descent. Kevin would be able to track them easily enough using his radio and other communication equipment, but he would have to tramp through the snow, and with the extra weight this would be energy sapping.

He was pleased to see that he was not the only member of the team that had strayed off course. Petty Officer Stuart Betts was close behind him and landed his parachute just a few metres away. Both of the men within the naval team proceeded to wrap up their parachutes and put all of their equipment in place for walking over to find the other members of the group.

Petty Officer Betts then looked at Kevin with distaste. Kevin raised his head after having stowed his chute to see Betts's expression, facing him with a loaded pistol and silencer pointed directly at him.

Kevin raised his hands and spoke calmly to Betts, "What are you doing?"

Betts replied, "None of your business; and you won't be requiring that equipment anymore."

Kevin went in for the rugby tackle head on, but before he could floor Betts into the snow and push the pistol out of his right hand, Betts pulled his index finger down on the trigger and it went off into Kevin's stomach.

Kevin slouched to one side and his face expressed an

exasperated picture of bewilderment. Betts was fully on his feet and let off two further rounds into the stunned man's abdomen, relieved him of his communication equipment and searched for the nearest cliff to push the body over.

CHAPTER 36

Betts ensured that his parachute was fully stowed in its accompanying bag, and that all the communication equipment that he needed was removed from the dead man's body.

He then proceeded to drag the body towards the large overhanging cliffs to the side of the glacier where they had landed. This was much harder than he could have imagined, with the thick powder snow, the weight of Kevin in all of his heavy survival clothing and the lack of grip for footholds on the steep side slopes of the Glacier de Bellecote.

Betts managed twenty metres before his breathing escalated to a level where he had to have a rest. Although the effects of altitude were slight, the exertion at this height made him desperate to have more oxygen and, as he was well aware, he was not becoming any younger.

Once he had had a couple of minutes rest and his breathing started to return to normal, the Petty Officer walked ahead to see where the best place would be to drag the body to before pushing it over the cliff. He found a spot where the cliff provided a sheer drop. This led to the bluish haze of an ice sheet, and below the ice was the visible wooded belt of trees that helped to span the valley between La Plagne and Les Arcs.

Betts then unhitched the coil of rope that he had been carrying with his parachute rucksack and tied this off to an upright, jagged rock adjoining the cliff face. He walked back down the slope and placed a coil of the rope under Kevin's arms and tied the loop off into a bowline. He had been taught the beginnings of the knot by a yachtsman he had met in his early days. "It's easy," he used to explain. "The bunny rabbit comes up out of its hole, goes along the field, around the tree and back down into its burrow." This in-built knowledge allowed Betts to complete the remainder of the rope work automatically.

Taking the loose end of the rope he walked up to the cliff edge and used the leverage of the rock to winch the body up to where he was standing. It was then an un-ceremonial pushover that sent Kevin tumbling, his body falling like a sack of potatoes in mid-air until it hit the ice-sheet. The collision with the ice-sheet saw the body being catapulted forward for several hundred metres before tumbling out of view.

It was time for Stuart Betts to report in, otherwise his current position may look even more suspicious than necessary. He pulled out his CB radio and checked that he was using the correct frequency.

"This is Comms. Seven, over, are you receiving?"

After what seemed like a long pause Archie replied, "Hearing you, Comms. Seven, state your position, over."

"Above Glacier de Bellecote ice-sheet, will meet you at intended rendezvous. Comms. Three has had a bad landing, over, I repeat a bad landing."

It was clear that Malcolm was surprised as the voice that came back whilst still authoritative, was slightly shaken:

"Bad landing noted, see you at rendezvous, 1200 hrs, out."

So Betts had approximately an hour to ski over to the original rendezvous located in the shadow of this mountain and protected from the stormy weather and higher winds. The good weather window was now closing and the cold front was pushing in with the wind starting to intensify. The sooner he was on his way the better.

This mountain had served him well; his mission was more

than on track and had already caused his leader rightful concern. Well, Lieutenant Archie Malcolm, there was going to be more of that concern, Betts thought. If Betts could influence the position, then Malcolm would not cope.

CHAPTER 37

Christoph led the French mountain rescue team that found the bright orange survival bag with the barely moving, three youngsters.

He did actually say *"mon dieu"* when he saw the sorrowful sight of the three students. All curled up as close as they were able, with Joseph and Emma wrapped around their younger brother Sam, although his ski pole splint and leg did not allow for people to lie in immediate close proximity to him. Christoph realised that these kids had been on the mountain for at least twelve hours too long.

His rescue team worked like a well oiled machine. Roles were automatically taken to place each of the three young adults into 'blood-wagons' to remove them from the mountain and back down to Plagne Centre as quickly as possible. The slope where the orange survival bag lay perched on the cliff edge and tangled in the jagged rocks was too steep and risky for a helicopter evacuation.

An expert skier would snow-plough their skis in front of the wagon with each hand holding onto a long wooden pole. The poles were connected to a stretcher behind, which lay on a couple of skids. They were extremely effective for removing patients from inaccessible areas of the region.

The rescuers had ensured that each of their captives were wrapped up properly for the journey and were comfortable. It would soon be discovered how dehydrated and in need of nourishment each of the skiers were. It was the role of the doctors in the resort town of La Plagne to provide the health check, following which they could make the right recommendations for casualties being brought off the mountains to be treated.

It was important that Sam's journey was smooth. His leg had become numb since the damage sustained on the rocks above the cliff edge. The rescue team decided to leave the temporary ski-pole splint in place, but worked around it to ensure that he would have as immobile a trip as possible, within a stretcher being brought down a steep glacier.

Emma's recollections of this period in her life, when brought round, were minimal.

She had lost track of time, and was confused by what had occurred over the last twenty four hours. She remembered being cold, oh so cold, like she had never been before. She would have given anything for a hot water bottle at that moment. She then remembered attempting to cuddle up to her brothers to share any body warmth that they had and Joseph humming James Bond theme tunes so that Sam would also attempt to hum along and not drift off into unconsciousness.

There was something else, and it kept ticking over in her mind, nagging at her. She just could not work out what it was. She attempted to take in her surroundings. Her whole close family was now around her and her parents were massively relieved that all three of their children were all going to be alright. Nothing had been anyone's fault and there was going to be no blaming, but her parents had been hugely worried and when they first saw Sam, they had only just managed to refrain from tears.

Joseph seemed to have braved the worst of it; he sat on the edge of a temporary bed in the hospital centre with a steaming hot drink in his hands. His eyes and whole face had lit up again. He was telling their parents how good the snow had been, how they had done justice to the powder at the very top of the off-piste; how it had been a freak hidden rock that had pulled Sam's ski away from his boot and then how the ski had rocketed over the cliff edge. Joseph did not mention the visitors that had been present prior to the French rescue team. He seemed to have forgotten about that episode within the story.

Emma was still mulling things over in her head and all of the bits just would not fit together. She was sure that Joseph had left their winter survival bag momentarily. Again, the times were unclear and, try as she might, the facts that she had would not straighten out. The one thing that was just weird and was unable to fit in the jigsaw was the voice of someone that she knew. My goodness, the voice of Archie Malcolm and what did he have to do with this mess. She went back to sleep. Sleep could only sort out the confusion and even if it did not, she knew that she really, really, needed it.

CHAPTER 38

It was twenty-four hours since the Woodcutter had received his Code Red message and he had had little sleep since. Try as he might to be overly busy, cooking his full fry-ups for breakfast, utilising the relaxation zone pool and sauna to put the events out of his mind, chopping as much wood as possible for the wood burner in the lounge area and carrying out general maintenance work on the chalet, the thought that the overall mission may be compromised was eating away at him.

His military training pointed him towards the direct action route. He had always reported back through to Portsmouth so it did make sense to go there and find out exactly what was going on. It was imperative that the overall mission was not compromised and that his family were safe.

As part of his military training, in abandoning a post, it was vital that no clues were left as to how that post had operated. Furthermore, if anyone hacked into the information that was retained on the hard drive of the computer systems within the first floor converted bedroom, many peoples' lives would be at stake. So there was much work to be done to ensure that the whole of the chalet would become just another holiday home.

The Woodcutter started to sensitively and painstakingly remove all of the gadgetry from the first floor converted bedroom. It was important to leave the room without any evidence of his having been there. He would wipe all surfaces, swab down the walls and areas behind where the computers had been installed. For now, all of the contents were being walked down to the basement and loaded into skidoo carrier compartments. He would then personally destroy what he could. A big fire would probably be best, he thought. A long distance from the chalet and then he would bury whatever had proved resistant to a good burning.

He determined that the equipment supplies for the chalet for the last few months and much of the winter clothing, climbing and skiing paraphernalia would have to be removed. If the chalet was going to be completely vacated within the next twenty-four hours then he needed to act fast.

He also checked the basement area to see if his emergency escape route was still all in place, and satisfied that it was, he proceeded to continue to clear out his communication hub. This had been the centre of his life for the last few months.

Before the light completely disappeared, he also wanted to allow time for a cross country ski around his favourite tracks, which would take in the wonderful views of this winter wilderness valley, with the Mont Blanc massif in the far distance. The chalet was always discreetly hidden, but he had become familiar with the lie of the land and how to best locate the building.

Once most of the internal works had been completed, he removed the thin cross country skis from their place within the basement store and put on his specialist walking/skiing boots that allowed the front straps of the skis to go over the toe area of the boots. As these were cross country skis, there were no click in bindings required for the back heels.

Skiing away from the chalet he sighed to himself and considered that he was nearly at the end of an interesting few months. Months that would shape his life forever, either for better or for worse. As he neared the Alpine forest closest to the chalet where some of the wildlife tracks began, he heard a very faint, small but unmistakeable noise. It was totally foreign in this still, alpine environment, yet totally clear.

It was a cough, and it had not been made by any animal that he knew.

CHAPTER 39

Archie and his team had eventually made it to the head of the wilderness valley that corresponded with all the details that had been on the original surveillance. Jackie and Jo had painstakingly memorised the lie of the land of this ten square mile patch.

Peering into their scopes, the steep contours of the higher mountain smoothed into the gentle roll of snow in front of them. Lower down, there were snow covered openings leading into the picturesque, pine forest that lay well away from any other habitation.

The dark brown of the trees, with their frosted tops and the steep hummocky slopes of the valley side, provided a secluded location and from where the team was currently lying, stretched out with their heads leaning forward for the best possible view, it was clear that if there was any activity within this valley, it was extremely discreet.

Archie was still coming to terms with the death of one of his team. Kevin, an experienced communications specialist and a veteran of similar parachute drops, should not have had any concerns with the landing. Yes, the plane had dropped them off course from the intended landing zone and yes, the conditions were far from ideal with an increasing wind and the onset of light snow before worsening conditions, but something felt odd about the course of events.

The remainder of the team, Nick and James as scouts, Jackie and Jo, Archie and eventually Stuart Betts had all made it to the original rendezvous, at the head of the valley beneath the Glacier de Bellecote. Stuart Betts had told them of the catastrophe that had met Kevin. That his chute had not opened fully and meant that he had veered off to the right-hand-side of the glacier. Stuart had attempted to increase the speed of his parachute to catch him up and bring him into safety on the mountain.

However, the wind had picked up, and taken Kevin faster and further to his death over the sheer rock cliffs where he then must have been thrown down the ice sheet to the pine forests below.

Archie had insisted that the group retrace the path as best they were able. The naval squad had eventually stood gazing from the rock cliffs to the ice sheet below. Could he see a faint trail of blood where the body had landed? It was not clear. There were the remains of the parachute, cut and shredded by the razor sharp rocks on the mountainside of the cliff edge. Blood was also visible on the parachute; Archie could not understand how it came to be on the parachute if Kevin had been below the material. Still, the wind could have whipped his body around, crashing him into the cliff, perhaps with part of the parachute below him when he was trying to land.

Team morale was dangerously low. Archie had increased the pace so that any valuable time lost on the initial landing and regrouping had been made up by their navigation to their current position. Jackie and Jo had come into their element. Having memorised the satellite positions where it was thought that communications were being made affecting the import and export position of the UK, both the girls had liaised closely with the scouts, Nick and James, to move the patrol via the most discreet and quickest routes.

This had involved the team skiing down to the top of the tree level and then following cross country tracks running within the highest sections of the pine forest. The patrol had then met the ridge that they were currently utilising. This was their viewpoint into the target valley. From here they could see the whole expanse of the valley, but it had not been easy climbing up to the ridge.

With full packs and limited rope, and attacked by the icy wind which was now strengthening dangerously, and with the weight of their mountaineer walking boots, the ascent up the rock gulley to the ridge had been difficult. The team had been reliant on every person working together to bring them all to the top. The ascent had slowed their progress and meant it was now late afternoon.

Archie was aware of how still and quiet it was. Stuart Betts seemed to be the one person in his team who could not sit still and, subconsciously, Archie's attention was being drawn to the man. Archie still did not entirely trust him. There was something furtive about his behaviour.

The Petty Officer's constant movements did not help Archie's concentration and it was at that moment that Petty Officer Betts coughed, and he coughed loudly; a bellowing, rasping cough. Archie just looked at him directly and quietly commanded, "Shut up, for the sake of us all and the mission."

CHAPTER 40

Emma woke from her long sleep. She yawned and stretched and blinked her eyes to move the effects of the previous twelve hours tucked up in her chalet bed.

The light was straining to pass through the flimsy blue coloured curtains and she could hear the shower running and the kettle straining its way to the boil.

"Mum," she yelled. "Are you up?"

"Do you want a cup of tea?" was the echoing response.

"Yes, please," Emma shouted and turned to the romance novel that she was reading.

Few people apart from her closest friends understood her passion for the romance books that she read like there was no tomorrow. Lost in the pages of Blair and his manly athletic torso; the hero was being reunited with his long lost childhood flame, Candy. Emma again thought about what had happened to her and her brothers over the past couple of days. It seemed like a lifetime ago now.

She had never been put through a situation like it. Her family experiences growing up had been positive and her mother and father and Joseph and Sam had always held each other together, through thick and thin. True, there had been instances that had been difficult. She homed in on one such time when it had been her birthday and her brothers had had a huge argument all day.

It had started over whose turn it was on the new computer game that had been bought. Joseph being the elder brother had picked up the black imposing controller with the large red buttons first and had insisted that he continue until all his

106

lives ran out. As he had shot the enemy successfully in the Rambo style game, achieving further penetration of the jungle in which the prisoners of war were being held, he had not wanted to hand over the controls.

As the game was new, for a reason she could not remember, there had not been an easy way to save his position. Sam had been sulking that it was his turn and had demanded that Joseph let him in on some of the action. Joseph, absorbed in his game, had ignored his younger, irritating brother and even when pushed to end his go by their mum, had steadfastly refused. For Joseph was just about to take out the main munitions bunker by a night air raid that lay behind the defences to the enemy jungle encampment.

Sam had started to cry, but then launched himself at Joseph to take over the controller. Joseph, still concentrating on the screen, had elbowed Sam out of the way whilst managing to bazooka part of the wall guarding the enemy encampment, to create an entry point for his men.

Somehow, both her brothers had ended up screaming at each other and rolling on the floor. Hitting each other mercilessly on the shoulders, stomach, and legs; anywhere but their opponent's head.

Their father had come in, broken them up and sent them to their bedrooms. They were both in "big trouble, and might have some time to reflect before their big sister's birthday tea".

Her birthday tea had been pretty muted as a result. Try as they might to lift the spirits of the whole family, with yummy cake, chocolate fingers, fun music, bright colours, jelly and ice cream, as her brothers were only answering in one syllable "yes" and "no" answers to how much they wanted to eat and not contributing to the conversation, it was a real dampener on her day.

This had been an exception to the normal routine of

growing up, she reflected. She was so lucky to be a part of a loving, caring, wonderful family and she strongly believed that this is what had pulled them through. It was what had kept them going through the awful cold of the mountainside, through the ever increasing doubt as to whether they were all going to make it back to their comfortable chalet, and to the warmth of their parents' faces as they were being reunited.

Now her mind turned on a different track, wandering, searching, to try and make sense still of those hours in the darkness. What had Archie Malcolm to do with it? That was a difficult one. Why did he keep cropping up in her half-sleep? Yes, he was fairly tall, pretty good-looking and athletic. Someone you admired and respected and trusted and, well...it was best not to dwell. Before her ordeal, she had been focusing on David anyway. She had had fun with David and had been able to chat freely. Archie was an enigma. She had never really had time to know what he was like, though the more she thought about it, the more she decided she wanted to find out about him. Just who was the real Archie Malcolm?

CHAPTER 41

Emma finally made it out of bed. She ruffled her crinkled brown curly hair and grabbed a dressing gown before padding in her new reindeer animal slipper socks through to the common area. The chalet had under-floor heating and the South African hosts had already been up and laid out breakfast as it was their day off. On the pine table was an assortment of jams, cereals, a couple of baguettes and clear instructions on how to use the dishwasher.

Her mum enquired, "Another cup of tea, then?"

"No thanks," said Emma, "I want to do justice to the mountains, despite our incident before we leave tomorrow…"

"You just take it easy, darling," her mum said. "We don't want you or your brothers any more exhausted than necessary."

"Fine, but I'm going to pop up to Plagne Centre for lunch and hit the pistes this afternoon," Emma reiterated.

"Well, seeing you are committed to it, I'm sure your father and Joseph will want to join you but I will stay put with Sam whilst his leg is recovering. I just want to keep a mothering eye on him."

Joseph and Emma's father appeared. They were both groggy eyed. As if in unison, they simultaneously went for the orange juice and the croissants piled up next to the baguettes.

"It's a good day," he said. "Are you planning on heading up to the pistes, Emma or … I hope you are going to rest a little?"

"I was just telling mum that it would be fun to leave La

Plagne on a high, even though we have been through such a traumatic experience. I need to find my skiing legs again."

"We understand Emma, but we should all go steadily. Let's look to catch the chair soon after midday."

"Sounds like a plan," Joseph chipped in and grabbed his towel so that he could go off and shower.

Emma buried herself again in her romantic novel. Candy was now more than happy in being reunited with her childhood sweetheart and thinking about some of the deep and meaningful aspects of life. Candy was already planning her future and a house for her and her partner. There was room for a whole family, a beautiful kitchen, a walk-in wardrobe and there would be a garden for them all to play in. Where would they live? Would it be by the sea, or in the forest, or close to the mountaintop?

Emma read on and on. She could only empathise with Candy. She wanted a perfect man but she knew that her friends had always criticised her for having such high standards. The right man will come along, they would say, but so far, she had just had many a good friendship and not felt secure enough to let any of those male friends into her close family life.

CHAPTER 42

With their minds made up to hit the La Plagne pistes in the afternoon, Emma, her father and Joseph went about it in style.

Joseph led the way on his twin tip skis with beautiful sweeping turns. Skiers dangling in the chair lifts above, or standing on the side of the piste, would stop and stare. Their eyes followed his line to admire the perfect turns and rare relaxed movements of someone who has been skiing since he was a toddler.

Emma did not need to compete with Joseph, for her movements outclassed those of her younger brother. Once Joseph had skied past any onlookers, the focus was solely on Emma, for she had the skill and the line of her brother, but she also oozed sophistication. What was beautiful about Emma was that she was innocent of it, for she loved every minute she was skiing. She was back in her dream world of exquisite happiness.

Their father had been an extremely skilled skier, but his movements did not flow as they once had.

The runs flew under all of their skis and it was only when Emma looked at her watch later in the afternoon, feeling a little tired, that she was shocked to see that it was nearly four o'clock and only fifteen minutes until last lifts.

Up they went to the top of the Roche de Mio, and then blasted down the runs all the way to Bellecote, catching the last link over to the La Plagne valley. What an afternoon! Confidence was restored with some beautiful awe inspiring runs incorporating amazing views across to Mont Blanc. These truly were excellent snow conditions with little ice, few loose rocks and quiet pistes. The family party revelled in the fact that they had not had to queue for any lifts the entire week.

Their afternoon was just what Emma, Joseph and her father needed after the emotional drain of the previous seventy-two hours. It had been the first time since the incident that Sam and his leg had been cast momentarily from their minds.

On returning to the chalet the family had ordered take-away food from the local pizzeria so that Sam would not have to hobble outside to the nearest restaurant.

The pizza went down well, with the local red wine and music blasting out from the CD-player, which sat adjacent to the roaring wood-burner.

Once the family had filled up on pizza, salad and chips, they retired to the comfy chairs around the fire.

Emma's father's favourite chalet game was *Jenga*. The tower of wooden blocks had to be extended each go by a player taking a wooden block from the existing tower, being careful to ensure that the tower did not topple onto the floor and putting the block onto the top of the tower to create the next level. A simple yet effective game. The family took it very seriously.

Whilst this was her father's favourite game the boys loved *Risk*. They did not necessarily want to take over the world, but it was always fun to do battle with each other, to see how their armies could grow by taking over territories and what tactics their opponent would play to stop them in their path of world domination.

Emma was itching to read the last few chapters of her romantic novel and see if Candy really did live happily ever after, or if there was a final twist. She was hoping that Candy was able to live her dream but the big what if was the potential for her previous lover to come back and spoil the fun.

Emma realised that they were also at the end of her holiday and, whilst it had been traumatic in many ways with the night on the mountain, it had brought her whole family closer together. She was uninspired by her student studying and where her geography course was taking her and was a little depressed about the thought of leaving this relatively un-spoilt, Alpine wilderness.

For some reason she couldn't quite fathom in her mind, her thoughts were also elsewhere with how she had talked to David on the Canadian canoe drifting down the River Wye. He was lovely, but there was something she was unsure about with him, something she could not place a finger on. Could she really trust him? And could she also trust Archie? Her mind was such a muddle. All she knew was that yes, she needed to understand and know Archie Malcolm better.

CHAPTER 43

David was seated at his small desk within his cramped student digs attempting to avert his gaze from the hall of residence window which gave him an excellent view of the end of the M275. This was the main gateway into Portsmouth. If he leant back in his seat he could glimpse the edge of the naval dockyard and the ferry port whisking their passengers across to St. Malo in France and Bilbao on the north coast of Spain.

Try as he might to focus on his engineering coursework, which was totally theory based for this semester, he could not concentrate. He just wanted to put the theory into practice.

David was a practical man. He loved configuring the elements required for an engineering machine to work. One of his highlights as a child, even though he was brought up in a number of homes, was a sponsored trip to the Science Museum in London.

This had been an exciting break to the standard routine. Whilst football was fun each week, London and the Science Museum was an unknown.

Having started life in East Anglia, everyone he knew had talked about the Big Smoke as another world, where glimmering office skyscrapers gave way to the pedestrian multitudes shopping at the beautiful high street shops and boutiques of the West End. They talked about the hordes of tourists viewing the sightseeing highlights, – the Tower of London and its Beefeaters, the imposing grandeur and austerity of Westminster Abbey, peering through the gates of Buckingham Palace from the Mall for a view of any of the

Royals. They had joked about feeding the pigeons in Trafalgar Square and perhaps daring to go on a scary trip into the London Dungeon or having an introduction to many of the world's most famous people at Madame Tussaud's. David had been able to play with miniature red London double-decker *Routemaster* buses and black London taxi cabs whilst a very young child, so the thought of seeing the real thing had given him palpable excitement.

To think that he was to be on a day trip where all of these activities lay only a stone's throw away had given David a focus. More importantly, their home was to be visiting the country's premier technical museum, which again had had wonderful reviews from everyone he knew.

David had not been disappointed. Staring at the exhibits, soaking in how a steam engine works, he could directly change the amount of water and fuel being provided to the engine and this was a thrill that he would never forget.

He had left the Science Museum with special memories and was even more determined to pursue a career as an engineer and solve practical problems through his ingenious mechanisms.

Any concentration that he had had for the textbook soon evaporated. He stood up from his desk chair and wandered down his third floor hall of residence bedroom corridor to the communal kitchen. He put the kettle on and hunted for some bacon that he was sure he had left in the fridge from the previous week. He smiled to himself, it was still there. It was rare in student halls for partially opened food to remain lying around, especially as he had not put a sticker on it with his name.

As his nostrils were taking in the delights of the bacon cooking, two of his corridor colleagues popped in.

"We need some more smoke, Davey. Can you sort us out some? Here's a twenty."

"Whoa, whoa, I'm really not the man, and you should be more careful than just casually asking me for this."

"But you so are the man, Davey, everyone knows that you can fix anything."

David huffed but pocketed the note and looked away from his two student colleagues. In the distance he could hear sirens. They were becoming louder and seemed to be heading for this central area of Portsmouth.

Just another day, they all thought, sirens were always going off in the centre of Portsmouth.

CHAPTER 44

The sirens grew closer to the hall of residence. It was the whooping sound of a couple of police cars. As they wove their way towards the student accommodation the decibels faded away and then reverberated twice as loudly as the sound tried to weave its way round the density of buildings within the commercial district of the city.

The students had nowhere to go, nowhere to hide or to run to. They stayed put like rabbits in headlights. After all, what was the worst that could happen, a fine, a caution?

Surprised that the police were actually coming to their halls of residence, David and his chums headed back to their respective bedrooms to remove anything incriminating.

The police cars pulled up outside, with the policemen heading directly to the hall reception. The officers had some urgency to their movements and their expressions were grave.

These were not the portly figures of many a Hollywood movie, but some of the cream of the police force, and they were acting purposefully. These vibes were picked up by the students. The police officers were confident in what they were doing, presumably tipped off as to illegal activities within the hall. The students were not used to such brazen tactics by Her Majesty's law and order.

David and his hall mates busily moved any illegal supplies that they might have had behind cupboards and into the common area lavatory cisterns of the third floor bathroom. David was determined that his extra income would not be cut short just yet. So far he was not known to the local police, except for his extra help as a comparable at identification parades. He was now on a mission to ensure that he appeared on the right side of the law with any spot checks that were imminent.

There was a mumbled discussion with the caretaker of the halls of residence which, despite craning their heads out of the kitchen windows, none of the students could make out. The police unit headed straight to the main staircase. David and his colleagues on the second floor were starting to perspire within their respective rooms. How had the police known that they were buying and selling illegal substances? Who had told them? How were they going to get out of this mess? Who could they blame or confirm as the main culprit?

The police unit went straight up to the second floor landing but did not take the staircase any higher. Heading along the corridor to their right, the first officer stopped outside room 2.24. On the nameplate in badly scrawled dark blue ink were the occupant details: "Richard Gupta," it read.

The first officer raised his clipped home-counties voice, "Please open your door, this is the police."

"Just a minute," was the response from within. After a couple more minutes the police reiterated their instructions but still there was no response from the other side of the bedroom door. A further siren could be heard within a couple of hundred metres and it was bearing down on the hall of residence.

The police unit had radioed down to plain clothes detectives to monitor the halls of residence from the outside. This would ensure that the goods that they had been tipped off about did not leave the building, out of their sight. Despite being on the second floor of this 1970s concrete block, it would not be too difficult for a young athletic student to make his way down to the ground floor using the exposed lintels and concrete beams which made up the exterior elevations of the property.

As Richard Gupta did not open the door, the police unit was forced to utilise their shoulder muscles against the piece of flimsy ply-wood in front of them.

The hinges fell away easily as the first officer used his strength to break through the doorway. The second officer piled into the room on his coattails. The student, appearing completely shocked, was standing adjacent to his wardrobe. Whilst Richard Gupta was detained and asked many searching questions about his recent activities, the remaining two officers starting trawling through his bedroom from top to bottom. In the first instance they found nothing. But they were not going to give up that easily.

Opening his exterior window, piled up on the small window ledge as far away from the bedroom as was possible, were at least twenty small but perfectly formed plants.

The two officers, who had been slightly disappointed from prising their way through every nook and cranny to find nothing, stopped and raised a smile at each other. The tip off had proved correct, both the men knew the memorable shape and style of those plant leaves.

CHAPTER 45

The bell-ringing tea was in full swing. Mavis was helping out behind the serving hatch of the village hall kitchen. She completed cutting the fifth slice of lemon drizzle cake with her thin plastic, gloved fingers and turned her attention to the next round of tea, which had just been called for.

There was a group of Tower Captains, situated close to the biscuit and sandwich table, discussing the merits of having more than one bell ringing tea a quarter, and the new additions to the district were busily utilising the hand-bells at the stage end of the hall.

Seated on three chairs, staring intently at each other, the Clackett sisters held a hand-bell in each hand. The sisters were in the midst of ringing a quarter peal on the six hand-bells held by the three of them. It was a quarter peal of spliced minor so, as each method was just about to come round, a call was made for the next method, whereupon the three ringers would continue onto yet another memorised pattern, always being sure to ring their bell at the right time whilst keeping the rhythm as steady as possible.

Such was the regular rhythm of their ringing, and the near perfect striking maintained over the full three quarters of an hour of the quarter peal, that the sisters had built up a crowd of local district members. Most of the members had pulled up a hall chair to form a small amphitheatre of spectators taking in the scene and quietly enjoying the spectacle.

At the other end of the hall were tables and chairs arranged for the tea in groups of four or six. These were currently partially filled, but being taken rapidly as ringers trooped in from having rung the bells within the adjacent St. Mary's tower.

David was helping out with the pre-tea ring and was standing in the ringing chamber calling the district ringers to order. Many of the ringers were still talking to each other and he had to raise his voice to be heard.

"All those who have not rung, please grab hold, let's ring some Plain Hunt with a half course of Yorkshire Major after that."

David took the seventh of the ring and took his place next to the Portsmouth Cathedral Tower Captain, who was ringing the tenor.

"We need to talk," he whispered.

"Not now," said the Tower Captain. "Let's go for a stroll after the ringing." He mumbled so quickly that none of the other ringers in the tower would have noticed that he had even spoken.

The Plain Hunt commenced and was a little lumpy as there were a number of learner ringers all finding their feet within the district ringing community and, whilst confident in their own tower, in unfamiliar surroundings their ringing was hesitant and did not flow.

Scowling and huffing and becoming agitated, for he was having to work harder than many of the ringers, being on the heaviest bell, the Portsmouth Tower Captain called "Rounds" and "Right, that's enough of that, David, c'mon, we're going to ring some Yorkshire Major now."

The Yorkshire Major produced a much higher quality of striking as only the better ringers knew the method. The natural rhythm and sound started to flow, and all who were involved drifted into the concentrated, dream-like state that typifies quality ringing from good bands. There was no shouting, pointing or directing. The ringers got on with it, and perhaps provided the odd nod or wink here and there, but the sound that was being produced was uplifting, joyful and inspiring.

The ringers brought the method to an end, ringing rounds prior to the Portsmouth Tower Captain calling, "Stand."

The Tower Captain again whispered to David, "Meet you outside in five minutes." David knew well not to ignore the request.

CHAPTER 46

In the aftermath of the fire on the freighter, Natalia and the few other passengers had been ushered into the one secure room that had not been affected by smoke: the bridge. Her brothers had not been found.

There was barely enough room for Natalia and her fellow travellers to sit on chairs within this control centre of the ship, let alone lie out and relax or actually go back to sleep.

It was a clear night, and the awesome Atlantic stars cast their light through the wooden-framed, salt-stained windows. Natalia's shadow detailed her fetal position pose. For such a formidable character it was a surprising demonstration of vulnerability.

The crew had now put out the fires and the strong odour of burnt wood and metal and plastics was starting to emanate throughout the remains of the passenger compartments. It was also permeating through to the games room area behind the bridge, and to where the remaining passengers were attempting to sleep.

The smell was tinged with other qualities, but few had experienced the mixture or recognized immediately what it was. All they knew was that it was a nauseous smell, and tried in vain to breathe through their mouths and block their nostrils off.

As dawn broke over the freighter, the Captain continued to check on his course for the day. He reviewed the speed in knots, the compass bearing and the weather forecast for the next couple of days. He needed his ship to be escorted into Portsmouth Harbour and for *The Islander* to have extensive repair work carried out prior to the next stage in her voyage.

He also needed to file his report on the fire and detail that Natalia's brothers were missing, presumed dead, but that no bodies had been recovered.

The ship was now cruising at three-quarters speed and would be on track to reach Portsmouth the following evening. The Captain was confident that no further repair works, apart from those to the passenger compartments, would be required. The engines and the hold had not been affected. Despite her current slumber, Natalia had also immediately asked the question whether the fire had spread to the hold of the ship. The Captain thought it strange at the time. Why should this passenger on his freighter be concerned as to what route the fire had taken?

It was imperative to Natalia that none of the Morales' stock had suffered from any effects of the fire. Even smoke damage would be a catastrophe. She had quizzed the Captain in detail as to where the fire had spread and where the smoke from the fire would have escaped to.

Fortunately for her and the remnants of her family, the Captain had confirmed that the whole ship was compartmentalised. As soon as the fire had broken out, the hold areas had been shut off and remained clear of fire and smoke. This had allowed Natalia to sleep. She was in no current state to absorb the horrors of the night. Having ascertained that her livelihood was safe, she fell into a deep sleep.

Once dawn had broken, and the sun had fully appeared above the horizon, shining its bright rays through the bridge windows, Natalia properly stirred from her slumber.

She recalled the events of the night and could not quite believe or recall her memories of what had happened. When she could remember enough to make sense of the events, it hit her that her brothers were not sleeping in the bridge with her and her fellow passengers and that they still had not been found.

She rushed so quickly to her feet that she felt light headed. She desperately scanned ahead for the Captain and realised that he was standing just a couple of metres away. She questioned where her brothers were. The Captain indicated that her brothers had still not been found and that the fire had been so intense that there was nothing left of the passenger compartments. She started shaking uncontrollably.

She had to have some air. Dashing out of the bridge door, she again attempted to focus her thoughts on the future. She focused on her life, her aspirations, and her dreams. She would start a new Morales family. Then maybe, someday, these events would prove themselves to be justifiable.

CHAPTER 47

The Islander was only an hour away from the approach to the Solent, the channel between the Isle of Wight and the mainland. The Captain had requested the standard tug escorts and the two smaller, powerful boats were to be with the freighter in a few minutes.

It was a fresh day with a clean autumnal wind blowing across the decks; enough to fly the flag from the mizzen mast.

Natalia was a mixture of emotion. Externally she was holding her feelings together, she had to, whilst internally her inner turmoil at losing her brothers and the responsibility that now weighed upon her was crushing, like an ever tightening vice. She was determined to lose the noose from around her neck, to shake off the shackles of what had happened, but it would take time as everything had occurred so suddenly.

Bournemouth had fallen into view and the freighter would soon be passing between Hurst Spit, the long sweep of pebbles which make up this intriguing coastal feature lying opposite the dramatic rock splinters of The Needles off the North Western shore of the Isle of Wight.

The crew were preparing the mooring lines and ensuring that the ship was ready for docking and unloading. The forty foot sea-containers were then designed to be removed extremely quickly prior to any loose items within the hold being packaged up and taken to the temporary storage warehouses in the port.

Natalia's cargo was a mixture of sea containers destined for homes further inland and smaller loose items which would be held in the storage warehouses. There was one particular container it was imperative she see with her own eyes.

Tucked away in the main hold was a non-descript cargo box, with few markings on the outside. It was registered to the port of Lima in Peru and its paperwork indicated that it consisted of a classic car and tribal craftwork. The tribal wares were a mixture of treated leather goods and woollens. The clothing and bedding material was to be distributed onwards across the UK and the classic car was to be low loaded to a specific address. This address was not anywhere within the freighter's paperwork and the addressee would protect his anonymity. Once the cargo had safely arrived Natalia had her precise instructions to follow. She had memorised the details in order that she could track the vehicle to its ultimate destination.

The freighter continued to make good progress past Fawley power station and the lights of Ryde with its prominent church spire jutting into view in the distance. The clearest landmark at this point was the Millennium Tower, completed four years after the Millennium in the shape of a huge spinnaker sail. The sail rose to an impressive height on the Portsmouth sea front overlooking the historic ships, the dockyard and the entire Southsea seafront.

Within the upper viewing deck of the Millennium Tower sail stood a non-descript middle-aged couple. Their view stretched along the entire Solent, across Gosport to the West and to the Downs of Hampshire. The couple had a wonderful view of the myriad of small craft and, as they were keen to take in all the comings and goings of the boats below them, they both wore high powered binoculars around their necks.

To all the other tourists on the viewing platform, they were just another everyday couple, possibly on holiday and, by their laughing and joking, definitely enjoying themselves.

As *The Islander* was identified by the lady, she gave a small nod to her companion, who raised a smile in return. Their boat and cargo were on track. Not needing to see anymore, the couple proceeded to the lower viewing deck and, having viewed the Solent, turned their attention to Old Portsmouth and the historic terraced streets beyond.

CHAPTER 48

David walked with a spring in his step. The ringing at St. Mary's tower and the tea had gone well. More importantly, he was now aware that he was going to be busy over the next few months and, as a result, would be paid generously. The advance he had received would more than compensate for any hardship or risk that he might face over the coming weeks.

The skip in his walk soon brought him to the junction of Southsea Common and the road back to his hall of residence. With an upswing in his mood he continued onto the tarmacadam path across Southsea Common that led directly to the seafront.

Children were playing football on the grass and there were a couple of families finishing off their lunchtime picnics. The planning and organisation for these family outings was evident. The mothers and fathers had been organised with all the necessary equipment, comprising rugs and hampers with an abundance of plastic cutlery and crockery. Many of the children appeared to be running wild with others attempting to fly kites.

One of the mothers was determined to read her *Heat* magazine and soak up the latest gossip of the Hollywood stars. Her youngest child was pulling at the edges of the magazine with his pudgy fingers in order to seek her attention. His pulling motion was becoming more and more desperate as she continued to be engrossed by the latest shenanigans of the many young famous people in her magazine. The stars were being featured in fabulous weddings, on their beach holidays, at play on the polo field and sipping champagne whilst at the races. There were some glorious settings and it took her a couple of seconds before she realised that her youngest son had just stepped in the leftover pudding and, in the same motion, ripped the back pages of her magazine.

Nearing the seafront, David gazed across at the imposing war memorial. It always reminded him of the history of the city and of the futility of war, with the high loss of life that resulted from every conflict. He was extremely grateful for his freedom and for not being tied to a particular regime or culture. He wanted to feel the benefits of capitalism and a free society, as to date he had not been able to afford any of life's luxuries.

Brought up in the various children's homes, there had been an abundance of clothing but nothing had been new. Toys had been donated, but often they were partly damaged or a few years old.

Having had his advance, it was the first time that he felt comfortable and free. He was ready to go on a shopping spree, to choose an item that he could now afford.

Strolling onto South Parade Pier, past the hustle and bustle of the brightly coloured amusement stalls and the haunted house blaring out its spooky music, David felt the sea air on his face and breathed in the slight smell of salt.

Squinting into the brightness of the far reaching horizon before turning to focus on the outline of the Isle of Wight, David saw the red flanks of the freighter. The freighter gave him goosebumps. Her name had been indistinguishable but the description that he had been passed matched the silhouette lying in the Solent. He stood and gazed at the conveyor of his future small fortune. She was going to allow him to live well and would be passing through the entrance to Portsmouth Harbour within the hour.

CHAPTER 49

The cough had been exaggerated and echoing due to the stillness of the air in the remote Alpine valley. The Woodcutter immediately remained put. What were humans doing out in this wilderness? Had his departure been compromised? He could only fear the worst.

Sinking to his knees in the snow he gently moved his ski boots out of the front ski bindings, lay spread-eagled on his outer jacket and salopettes, and put his ear to the ground and waited.

It was not long before he was rewarded.

The cough continued and, whilst there were attempts to muffle the sound, the reverberations allowed the Woodcutter to pinpoint the stranger's location. Up on the ridge above the Woodcutter's retreat, the interloper would have a view of all the comings and goings across the whole valley. Was there just the one individual or did he have friends?

Hiding in the trees, the Woodcutter considered that he was currently in the best location to remain undiscovered. He had completed the removal of all sensitive information from the chalet and now needed to cover as much distance away from his beautiful valley. He sighed; fate would play a part, for his means of escape was tucked up in the basement area of his retreat.

Speed and stealth were of the essence as the light was starting to go. He would climb far up the valley within the trees and then make a mad dash for his discreetly located property. If he was spotted and the contact was unfriendly, then he was well aware he would just have to fight it out.

There appeared to be no further movement. He took a good gulp of hot liquid from his flask, ate the last of his chocolate, and resigned himself to an interesting couple of hours.

The sun disappeared below the mountain ridge and the pink tinge swept across to the tops of the valley sides. He squinted and could not believe his luck. The strangers had remained on the ridge top and their tiny silhouettes were visible. They were lying on the ground and staring intently down the valley towards him but had not counted on his view, with the sun outlining their position so clearly.

He gulped as he was attempting to remove the bad taste from his throat. It had not been caused from the effort of having to cross-country ski upwards through the trees as quietly as possible, with minimum disturbance. He had counted six head shapes. It was at least five too many. He was trying not to let his dismay compromise his ability to think clearly.

He was certain that it had to be a military team. Friends just do not hang about on Alpine ridges after the sun has set in remote wilderness valleys that are tucked away from any towns, communication or habitation. His only chance would be the element of surprise. Certain that the team was not aware of him, but that he was aware of them, he had to use this knowledge to his advantage.

CHAPTER 50

Archie wanted some sign of movement within the wilderness valley beyond him. The cool mountain air was doing its best to invade the slight space between the back of his neck and his outer winter jacket. The ground was firm. Far too firm, as his muscles ached from having lain on this ridge for what felt like an eternity. There was the slight smell of dried human perspiration, but no other scent in this clean and clear and now slightly chill air.

Stuart Betts still shuffled beside him. Selfish and not caring for the group's mission, he had coughed audibly like a mountain gorilla. When he had tried in vain to muffle the sound, the Non-Commissioned Officer had only made the situation worse. Archie could not forgive him if that stupid cough had compromised his mission.

The mission, he pondered. Jackie and Jo had enabled the whole team to stay in line with the mission brief and their capabilities on the mountainside would be fully reported back to the Commander. Nick and James had also acted well as scouts. To say it was unfortunate that Kevin had met his demise was an understatement. There would be an internal investigation when the team was back at base. These events did happen. They were part and parcel of this kind of mission. Archie just was not convinced that everything was as it had been reported by Petty Officer Stuart Betts. There was something that the Petty Officer was withholding.

The light was starting to fade rapidly and the pink hues were beginning to appear on the mountaintops opposite. It was beautiful, but something else had suddenly caught Archie's attention.

In the far distance, a branch moved unnaturally in this still, late afternoon. Archie signalled instructions to the whole of his team who became alert and ready to move. The scouts had already begun creeping round to the pre-determined forward positions on each side of the valley. Jackie and Jo were going with Archie to the halfway point and Stuart Betts would remain on communications to keep the team together.

Archie viewed a gloved hand through his binoculars and then in a flash a whole figure appeared in cross country skiing motion. The figure was moving as quickly as was practically possible. The arms utilising the ski poles with all their might to push off the ground for extra movement and the picture of this briskly skating figure brought Archie to a few instant conclusions.

One, this was a strong, fit individual. Two, Archie assumed that he had spotted him and his team on the ridge. Three, the man was in a rush and would not be around long. Four, if Archie and his team did not intercept this man then their surveillance was likely to have been worthless. In conclusion, this was it.

Archie and the girls strapped their skis on and with a whoosh were off down the mountain. They each put in some impressive turns before re-grouping above their halfway point. But their movements had not gone unnoticed. The figure, now not so far in the distance, had even more obvious urgency to his skating stance.

Archie did not allow himself or Jackie and Jo to stop for more than a couple of seconds. His skis grated over some solid rock and some twigs and other debris were shooting up from under his teammate's skis. The pace was on; he felt perspiration down his forehead, under his arms, down the back of his neck. He must not let this man get away.

134

He saw above to his right and left James and Nick completing the pincer movement by flying down the off-piste. He was impressed by their style and speed. Over fifteen seconds, each of his scouts had dropped half of the altitude from the ridgeline and rapidly approached the loan figure heading for what appeared to be just another rise of snow in the hillside.

A couple of turns later and Archie's picture of the hillside rapidly changed. He saw the roofline, he gauged the size of the tucked away chalet and he needed to rapidly reassess the situation.

Who was going to make it to the building first? Did the cross country skier have accomplices? Archie's previous intelligence indicated not, but Archie knew from experience that it was unwise to completely rely on intelligence.

Once the cross country skier was on level snow and out of the trees he was on fire, as if someone had fitted a power pack to his back. Even Archie's scouts were going to have difficulty catching him. There was only one thing for it and Archie was now in range. He lifted his rifle to his shoulder and fired.

CHAPTER 51

Archie's shot went wide of the mark. The snow spat in the ground a couple of metres past the right shoulder of the cross country skier. The skier did not turn around, stop or change his course. Instead, he skied harder and faster with military precision.

The ridge of snow in front of Archie's team partially blocked their sight lines. James and Nick lifted their rifles to bear down on the skier. Nick's shot nicked the right calf of the figure and he could be seen staggering forward before becoming hidden behind the small snow ridge. Archie, Jackie and Jo, and the two scouts were skiing as quickly as they all could, to meet above the rise in the snow and take in the property that was hidden below.

Their intelligence had been unable to identify any permanent structures, let alone a full skiing chalet within this valley. Tucked into the hillside, with reflective materials and perfectly matching the lay of the land, Archie realised that this was the location that they had been searching for. The team had managed to find the hideaway from which covert signals had been emitted. Archie and his squad now just needed to uproot the skiing figure that they had spotted moments before, pin him down, and find out what was going on.

Penetrating the still air was the sound of a small motor. Archie, Jackie and Jo and Nick and James all stared at each other with alarm. It sounded similar to a lawn mower but was not an engine or noise that any of the team recognised.

Betts came in on the radio, "Perhaps he has a skidoo in the

basement. Suggest surrounding the property on the western flank before he has a chance of making it to the forest."

Archie thought this sounded likely. At last, a sensible suggestion from Betts, which might allow him to redeem himself. Archie signalled to the team to head to the western flank but for James to cover the eastern aspect in case it was a decoy.

Betts had taken in the plan for surrounding the chalet and skied down off his perch heading for the eastern side of the property. The motor noise became audibly louder and started to hum throughout the valley.

Whilst James had been ordered to cover the eastern elevation of the property, it was clear that the motor noise was loudest on the southern side, just round the corner from where he presently stood. James scrambled across the snow, in time to witness the basement wall electronically lower and transform into a small ramp. Inside, the Woodcutter was rapidly casting diesel over the whole of the basement area and carefully eyeing up his means of escape.

Betts was now standing close to James, who had grabbed his rifle and was attempting to puncture the chassis and the wings of the flimsy aircraft he had spied within and to hit the Woodcutter who was crouched behind the ramp. Both Betts and James were out of view of the other members of Archie's team standing on the western side of the chalet.

"Oh no you don't!" shouted Betts and picked up his own rifle which, instead of pointing at the pilot of the micro-light, he pointed at James.

"Put your gun down," Betts said calmly.

James could not believe what was going on. Betts was still holding a loaded rifle up at him and the micro-light was just about to take-off. The Woodcutter returned pistol shots from the micro-light's ramp trapping James where he stood. Betts took the opportunity to let off the rifle into his teammate. James fell forward and clutched his stomach in agony.

Meanwhile the Woodcutter said to himself, "Well, it's now or never," and jumped into the small framed chassis of the micro-light before hitting the throttle to maximum rpm for take-off. The small aerial machine sprung to life and quickly gained pace before hitting the ramp, leading the Woodcutter and his pride and joy into the open air beyond. The engine strained as she pulled away from the ground, projected by the ramp into the valley.

Archie looked in disbelief as part of the southern elevation of the property opened up. In the next moment, a micro-light was bouncing up the ramp to take off. The figure within the micro-light hurled a glass bottle towards the basement behind him causing the whole of the basement to explode into a cauldron of fire whilst firing a pistol from the cockpit of his aerial machine.

The micro-light bore away into the half-light of the valley. The remaining members of the team started to fire at the small, light aircraft from the western side, and continued until she flew out of range.

Eventually, the sounds in the valley softened to a near silence, only being interrupted by the gentle crackle of fire still being fed by the remains of the chalet. All the faces of the team were lit up by the warm glow of the flames.

CHAPTER 52

Archie twirled around in amazement as the micro-light flew off the ramp into the thin air beyond. With Jackie and Jo and Nick, the team had sought to bring the aircraft down with their military rifles. Whilst a few of the shots managed to pierce the chassis of the micro-light, the machine dodged and dived and turned sharply towards the other side of the chalet.

Archie and his team heard the crack of pistol shots emanating from the craft and ran to help James and Stuart Betts who had been firing up at the plane. As they ran round to support their colleagues Archie was shocked that James appeared to have been shot in the stomach. As he howled in agony the micro-light was already approaching the maximum range of their rifles.

The micro-light pilot semi-stalled the controls so that the aircraft glided sharply downwards on its own momentum and the remainder of the rifle shots flew over the top. She now started to ascend above the pine forest before disappearing as a tiny black fleck in the distance.

Archie had not planned for this escape. Whilst he had had the team surrounding the chalet and could have staked out the man who had fled from the forest on his cross country skis, the aerial craft had come from nowhere.

As quickly as the man had skied up from the forest into the hidden chalet, he had engineered what could only be considered an impressive departure. Archie and his team would have to salvage what they could.

The chalet was smouldering away from the diesel oil fire created by the small glass fuel bomb, but no part of what the fugitive had left behind would go unturned. The property had to reveal to Archie and his team a clue as to who this man was, what he represented, and to where he may have fled.

The flames would soon eat away at the remainder of the structure, so Archie shouted to Betts to look after James. Betts swiftly obliged and James seemed to howl even louder, but it was impossible to make out any clear sounds through the gurgling noises that were coming up from his throat.

Archie led Jackie and Jo and Nick into the front of the property, part of which had now fallen away to give them access directly onto the main staircase leading to the common area and bedrooms beyond.

The team scrambled throughout the chalet, breathing heavily with their exertion, yet shielding their faces from the heat of the flames. Archie racked his head as to where any clues could be found. Rather than dash around like a headless chicken, he attempted to focus strategically on routing through all of the areas that were still in one piece.

Archie sent Jackie and Jo to search through the upstairs bedrooms and Nick to go through what was left of the basement areas. Meanwhile he rapidly began hunting through the main living area. Normally, he would have been impressed by the exercise and chill out zone with the sauna and jacuzzi. Now, it was just a case of what might be unearthed from them. What secrets lay behind this luxurious setting and the objects that lay within?

In routing through the kitchen area, he went back to the cutlery draw and examined all of the utensils. The occupant had cleared out in a rush and had not fully had time to wash up his most recent meal. He put a couple of items of the recently used cutlery in a clear perspex sandwich bag.

Meanwhile, Jackie and Jo came back down the stairs looking disappointed and once they had helped Archie in the main living area, the three of them proceeded to the basement area.

The smoke from the fire was starting to billow up the main staircase and the three adults crouched low, holding material against their faces to shroud the worst effects of the fumes.

Nick appeared with a smile on his face. Could it be good news, Archie wondered? Nick approached Archie, held out his hand and calmly said, "Look at this."

Jackie, Jo and Archie peered through the murky air to see what Nick was holding. He held aloft a historic ships visitor pass, although slightly burnt it was clear that it was the historic ships that Archie was more than familiar with. Secondly, which had to be the icing on the cake, the previous occupant had left behind the remains of an address on the other side of the paper. Archie was sure that the digits that remained indicated an address in Southsea, of all places, but it would take some work from him and his team to track this one down. Flabbergasted and slightly bemused, Archie, Nick and the girls rushed out of the chalet, just as the fire began to lick up the main stairwell through to the common area.

CHAPTER 53

Archie called in the helicopter to take them back to the UK and the pick-up was arranged using two discreet sentences. The team was to head down the valley on their cross country skis for it was now dark and too cold to stay put.

James had succumbed to his wounds, forcing the team to bury his body next to what was left of the chalet. With limited time, the team honoured James in silence, putting him into a makeshift grave as quickly as they could. Whilst the smoke had eased, it still drifted skywards. The flames had died down to reveal the concrete frame but the majority of the wood had succumbed to the crackling feast of the fire.

The chalet was lit up and the authorities would soon be on their way to investigate the constant plume of smoke in this wilderness valley. Unaware of permanent habitation, they would be keen to ensure that their local environment was not being damaged by a forest fire.

Archie's team arrived at the tree line. He grunted instructions and Jackie, followed soon after by Jo, continued swiftly on. Jackie had ensured that she was on the right bearing and that Jo was ready for the pace to pick up. They had to temporarily remove James from their minds.

With the limited vision provided by their head torches, the girls stepped out in their cross country skis, making substantial progress over the rough terrain during the next gruelling couple of hours. Archie, Nick and Petty Officer Betts had viewed the diminishing flames from the tree line. There was no sign of others having been alerted just yet. Their team then similarly worked hard over the rough pine forest tracks through to the pre-planned opening in the trees. This provided the helicopter with its natural and discreet landing pad.

The air was sharp with the coolness of the night. The stars were bright in this alpine environment and the smell of the pine was overwhelming. The swish and swoosh of the blades was heard well before the helicopter appeared as a dark, ominous shape. As the craft landed within the clearing and the pilot flung open the side door, Petty Officer Betts pointed his rifle at Lieutenant Archie Malcolm and then swung it lazily towards the pilot.

"Stand back," he shouted above the roar of the displaced air caused by the down draft of the blades.

Betts clambered aboard the helicopter still pointing his weapon viciously at the pilot and then toting it towards Jackie and Jo, Nick and Archie. Archie raised his hands and just stated calmly, "Don't do anything stupid, Betts, you'll be hunted down and swing for this, you do realise that?"

Betts indicated to the pilot with his pistol to take off, and bring the chopper up and out of the trees. The blades rotated at a wilder speed and the engine's volume went up a notch.

"See ya in hell," shouted Betts as the helicopter's two stands edged away from the ground.

Nick dashed forward and threw his body onto the main deck of the mechanical beast, wedging his shoulder against the door frame to ensure that it remained open.

He was unable to push up with his legs and put anymore of his body into the helicopter. Betts pressed on Nick's hands with the full weight of his body but Nick was too fast for him and managed to lift his left arm up and gain a grip on Betts' right ankle. Not daring to move his other leg Betts brought down the full force of the back of the pistol onto Nick's head and this knocked Nick's head limply to one side.

The helicopter finally took off from the ground with Nick

still dangling out of the door, and most of his weight pulling through his left arm at Betts' leg and lower body.

The helicopter had gained a good fifty metres in height and each man was fighting to ensure that they did not leave the relative safety of the flying machine.

Betts' superior weight position allowed him to hit Nick's head a further couple of times with the pistol and, dazed by the ferocity of the attack, Nick's grip on Betts's ankle loosened. Betts kicked Nick's body with his free leg and turned away quickly into the body of the helicopter.

Archie watched in the half-light as the shape of a body fell over a hundred metres. With a thump, he heard it come to rest in the depths of the pine forest.

Nick lay very still with open, but not seeing, eyes. His body was looking up at the stars, a couple of kilometres from where Archie was standing with Jackie and Jo.

CHAPTER 54

Commander Edgar Bennett disdainfully picked up Lieutenant Archie Malcolm's report and shuffled the pages between the palms of his creased hands before placing the stack of paper neatly onto the leather topped writing desk that lay between the two men.

"It doesn't make for good reading, does it Lieutenant?" The Commander struck a formal tone.

"No, sir, it does not," said Archie, going for the less is more approach.

He knew when the Commander was royally annoyed and this was certainly one of those occasions. Archie could tell what the position was as he, too, was also more than frustrated at the course of events that had taken place in the French Alps.

He did not expect the next few moments, however. The Commander continued, "I had expected more, Lieutenant, much more."

"Yes, sir." Archie paused for breath and then stated, "We are now in a position to follow up specific leads received to ensure that both the inhabitant of the chalet and Petty Officer Stuart Betts are found and questioned."

"Lieutenant, I will be running this operation separately from now on. It is unfortunate, but you will be having no further involvement, is that understood?"

Shocked, and not for the first time in the last forty-eight hours, Archie could only confirm "Yes, sir." It really was not worth arguing in his tired and depressed state.

Once the full debrief had taken place, although Archie

emphasised that there was not much more to say than in his written report, Archie sought to remove himself from the naval base as quickly and quietly as possible.

Monica peered up from behind the sweeping curved reception desk on his way out. "See you, Lieutenant," she said cheerily, which raised a half smile from Archie in return. He was not able to manage more.

Practically running out past the sentries with his leather hold-all clutched under his arm, Archie decided that he desperately needed a break. There were other thoughts on his mind and people that he had not seen recently.

He wanted to catch up with Emma, David and his bell-ringing group. It had to do him good to be away from the mission, the debrief from the Commander meant his current spirits could not sink any lower.

CHAPTER 55

On leaving the naval base, Archie headed straight for his flat at Gunwharf Quays on the seafront. Letting himself in, he put on some soothing music, a Jack Johnson CD that he always listened to when he wanted to relax. His upbeat eighties pop music classics were for when he was in a doing mood. This music was calm and allowed him to reflect.

He grabbed a towel and enjoyed a hot shower with the music still floating through to his cleanly rinsed ears. He always remembered to wash behind the ears otherwise his mother would not have been happy, before changing into smart casual clothes. These were clothes in which he could try and forget the events of the day.

The flat had a small balcony and Archie pulled up the black side handle, which allowed him to open fully the sliding doors. He stepped out onto the wooden decking that, suspended at this height, gave a wonderful view onto the happenings of the Portsmouth Harbour entrance below.

Standing with the first glass of lager in his hand, Archie took in the view; the small sailing dinghies bobbing up and down on the large ocean waves with their strong tidal pull, the more substantial yachts mainly returning from their day's outings and the continual hubbub of ferries taking cars and passengers both to the Isle of Wight and the Continent.

Try as he might, the images of the torn parachute down below the sheer cliff edge belonging to Kevin, his communications specialist, the grimacing figure of James clutching his stomach; and the thud of Nick's body crashing to the ground from the helicopter above were preoccupying his thoughts.

These negative images were pervading his senses, consuming his mind and eating away at his sanity. His pint glass was still over half full but his soul was concentrating on the element that was empty. Archie knew that he was in trouble. He recognised that he needed to be in the companionship of his friends and groups that lifted his spirits. He just could not dwell on the events of the last few days. It would send him mad.

Yet again he wondered as to why Emma had been on the mountainside in the bright orange survival bag. What had she been doing there in the first place? She must never know that he and his team had been out on a mission. He was truly scared that something in her subconscious may pinpoint Archie and his band as having been by her side in the night. He needed to approach this one carefully. He had to ensure that Emma had no memory of that awful period.

What would raise his spirits? Well, certainly a walk out and about. He could not mull on all that had slipped from their grasp. Where was Petty Officer Betts now? What had happened to the cross country skier who escaped from his secret alpine chalet in a micro-light?

Anyone would have thought it ridiculous. Quite a story you have there, Archie, they'd laugh. It wasn't a laugh, though, was it? It had cost the lives of three of his close team. The perpetrators were still out there, somewhere, and yet he, Lieutenant Archie Malcolm, had achieved nothing. Furthermore, he had been taken off the mission, which had been his only chance of redeeming himself, of fighting on and proving the Commander wrong and ensuring that all the culprits were brought to justice.

He finished off the cool lager, closed up the sliding door and picked up his wallet, mobile and keys from the round wooden bowl on the side table by the front door of his flat. He could not help himself from slamming the door on his way out as he was so annoyed. He could not stop the ideas, the conflicting thoughts, from swimming around his confused and aching head. He needed the fresh air, the effects of the endless sea horizon and the interaction with friends to distract his mind and wholly absorb him in something, anything, else.

CHAPTER 56

Archie absorbed the view from the Hard. This was where Portsmouth had originally been fortified. Admiral Lord Nelson himself had visited this area of Portsmouth many times. Steeped in history, it was from the Hard that the pilgrims had set sail to the Americas on *The Mayflower*.

The fishermen were in their usual place, casting their lines off the small raised jetty to the left, and this was above the isolated pebbled beach where he was standing. As this natural, sea-ravaged part of the coast was surrounded by the thick walls of the Portsmouth ramparts, it was a sun trap in the summer months. Students revising for their exams were attracted here, as were many more who just sought to soak up the sun. It was too cold for anyone to be lazing on the beach today but there were a handful of dog walkers, joggers and old age pensioners breathing in the sea air.

Archie climbed up the stone staircase so that he could walk along the sea defences where roller-bladers, cyclists in the new cycle lane, and walkers were going about their business. This route took him along to South Parade Pier. It gave his mind some air to refresh his thought patterns. Despite it now being the onset of spring, the water was still cold so he was impressed to see so many sailing craft out of their marina berths.

Even more impressive to Archie was the group of windsurfers rapidly flying across the surface of the waves, skimming above the water and somehow managing to stay dry as they shot across.

Their boards appeared to be impossibly small compared with the size of the rigs that drove them forward. The wind would force the rig back and down and to increase the speed further the windsurfer, leaning out from the board by using his harness, normally strapped around his bottom and attached by a hook to the harness loop on the horizontal boom, would close the slot of the gap between the bottom of the sail and the board.

Like a streamlined car, with no roof rack or unsightly extremities to cause drag, the windsurfer and his board would then really fly. So much so that, to stay on the boards, the designers had to introduce foot straps in order to ensure that the windsurfer was not completely dislodged by a wave or just by a slipped foot.

Conversely, it always amused the windsurfers themselves and those watching if a previously strong wind just died to nothing. The windsurfer closing the slot with his body fully out from his board, using his harness with feet secured in his foot straps would suddenly find himself being taken by gravity into the water.

Try as he desperately might to pull on the boom and reach for the mast, normally there would be no recurrence of wind to keep him upright. The observers from the shore and the other sailors would see the hilarious sight of a windsurfer momentarily freefalling backwards into the water with nothing to save his descent. Both board and sail would be going so quickly that the body would fall like a stone directly downwards whilst his board, sail and boom would continue sailing on for ten or twenty metres forward.

Archie checked his watch and it was still only late afternoon. He had the aftertaste of the lager on his tongue and he was starting to feel a little refreshed from taking in the activity of the coastline.

Continuing to walk along the promenade he was aware

that he was level with the Royal Marines Museum and their adjacent former barracks, now converted into high quality houses and apartments.

Having walked this far and checking the time, he realised that he could watch the end of the water-polo team practice in Eastney pool. When Archie had shared the house with David, David had attempted to coax him along to the water-polo training sessions. Whilst Archie enjoyed the fun of the competition, most of the swimmers were extremely strong.

Even Archie was aware that the team was better without his contribution. Still, he could see how his ex-house mates were doing and if they were going for a quick drink after training.

Popping into the steamy atmosphere of the 1950s swimming baths he passed through the spectators' side door, located a couple of steps down from the back of the car park. He sat down on the wooden slatted bench and slid into the centre, trying to cause little disturbance to the training session.

David had the water-polo ball in his hand and lifted it up and over his head and drove it with impressive force, using the palm, towards the other side's goal. The goalie did well to block the shot and the ball was deflected up to where Archie was sitting.

David noticed Archie on the side and raised a hand, mouthing that it was five minutes until the end of the session. Archie continued to watch and was staggered by the speed of the movement, the fitness of the teams and the camaraderie amongst the teammates.

Eventually the whistle sounded. David's team had won by one goal and he swam over to the side where Archie sat.

"We're going to the Winford Inn off Palmerston Road," he shouted above the hum of the lights. See ya there in thirty minutes, or if you want a lift we'll be leaving from the car park in ten."

"No worries," replied Archie. "I'll catch you guys in half an hour – some impressive shooting there."

"Thanks," David responded and popped off to the changing room.

CHAPTER 57

The Winford Inn off Palmerston Road, Southsea, was a typical student drinking den.

One of the hockey teams was already standing around the bar. There was a rush to order the jugs of lager before happy hour came to a close. In essence the students were receiving four pints for the price of three so they were keen to line up their drinks. The bar staff were having difficulty keeping up and the landlord promptly rang the bell to indicate his establishment was taking last happy hour orders.

Many of the students were scrambling around for any spare pennies in their pockets. They were attempting to pool together to see if they had enough money between them for another jug, or alternatively whether their group would hit the pool table or the quiz machine.

A couple of locals were enjoying the comfort of the cushioned corner seats and discussing the merits of the new European player who had been bought for a phenomenal sum for their local football team. Would this one player make the impact that they needed? Expectations were high. The player had to perform to ensure their team remained out of the relegation zone.

In the restaurant, connected by the archway that had been knocked through a couple of years ago to create this dining extension, and delineated by more modern laminate flooring instead of the traditional large paving slabs, there were a couple of parties who were finishing up their late, three course lunches.

Some students had their parents to visit for the weekend.

In order that they could have a decent meal, courtesy of their parents, and exchange information about their life in Portsmouth for the most recent family news, the Winford made for a reliable location.

Archie had managed to order a pitcher of the happy hour lager and was reading through the local newspaper. There was no breaking news, just the usual local parliamentary candidates views, moaning about rubbish collection rates and car crime and the worrying trend of increased vandalism depressing further the existing poor state of the retail high street. With nothing grabbing his attention, Archie looked up and was pleased to see David enter with a small group from the water-polo team.

David headed over to Archie and Archie offered him a drink from the pitcher. It felt like old times when they had shared a house together. David was attempting to clear his nose as the chlorine in the swimming pool water had irritated his eyes and he sneezed. Archie asked him how he was and what David was up to. David seemed a little shifty. He went through what he was studying on his engineering degree, confirming that he was not enjoying this semester as there was far too much theory and not enough practical. He mentioned that he was still living in the hall of residence in the city centre as a senior student and was still playing mixed hockey, water-polo and bell-ringing at St. Mary's regularly.

Archie congratulated David on the St. Mary's striking contest win and asked him if he had seen Emma recently. David blurted out that Emma was popping over to the pub in the next ten minutes or so, and that they were going to the Athletics Union Ball the following night.

Many male students thought Emma extremely attractive and her house on Kent Road in Southsea was one that most of the guys on her course would be thinking up excuses to visit. With her slightly curly brown locks, and slim yet curvy figure she was very popular. In addition, her kind and caring nature and positive outlook on life ensured that those who spent time with her enjoyed the company. These natural qualities made people fall in love with Emma.

"Oh," said Archie, "that will be nice for you."

"It sure will," said David, "you know I'm thinking about asking Emma to move in with me."

The conversation became strained and Archie could not concentrate again. David and Emma's friendship appeared to have progressed to something more since his birthday Canadian canoeing on the River Wye.

Archie was going to the Athletics Union Ball anyway as he was well known in student social circles. As his front was that he was undertaking PhD work in connection with oceanography, he did not have a readily available crowd to go with but he'd been looking forward to catching up with Emma and David. He was now not sure whether he wanted to go and see two of his best friends together. One whom he had known for years and one much more recent, but he did not want to see them as a couple, it was not right.

Archie wished David well, confirmed he had to finish off writing up yet another part of his research analysis, and that he would see them both the following night at the Student Union.

CHAPTER 58

Archie stood tall and gazed around the room. His black tie meant he appeared dapper. He certainly did not stand out like a pompous penguin. He was handsome anyway, so there was more than one look in his direction from the ladies. All the guys had scrubbed up and it certainly made for a change to see the rugby, football, cricket, athletics and water sports teams in smart clothing.

Many of the men could not resist the urge to gawp at the ladies. The girls they played mixed hockey with, or who they had good banter with once they had finished their netball matches appeared as completely different, stunning people.

David was in his element for a couple of reasons. One, he thought he had the most beautiful girl at the university standing by his side and two, he was now able to do business in a big way and this was just the start. His calculations had confirmed that he would make a large amount of money by the end of this one evening. More than he had previously made all year.

Archie walked around the main hall of the union which had been entirely transformed for this surprisingly grand annual event. There was a bucking bronco mechanical bull in the corner surrounded by inflatable bouncy castle material. The bull was sited next to a miniature casino, which was adjacent to a game Archie had never seen before. It looked fun.

Down three inflatable alleyways contestants would run forward, pulling against a bungee cord strapped around their waists that attempted to bounce them back to where they had started. The object was to run as far down the alleyway with as much speed and momentum as possible, propelling yourself forward to reach one of the cowboy hats placed at the end of the alleyways. It was hilarious to see all of these sportspeople giving it their all, just to be bounced all the way back to where they had started from without having grabbed the prized cowboy hat. Coming back down the alleyway with a cowboy hat would win a prize and there were some attractive prizes on offer. These included a meal for two at a top restaurant, a speedboat ride in the Solent, or a free trip round one of the Premiership football stadiums. There was a good sized queue to have a go and Archie could not resist joining it.

Meanwhile, David enjoyed Emma's company, although her mind seemed to be elsewhere. All of David's friends had commented how lucky he was to be there with Emma. He could only agree. Emma's simple yet sophisticated style just enhanced her natural beauty.

Normally she did not dress up, and now she had she could not help but turn heads. She was wearing a short purple dress with matching shoes, a neck ribbon of similar colour and a pendant that had been given to her by her mother when they had been shopping in Wimbledon, for doing well in her A-Levels. She wore a minimal amount of make-up, just enough to highlight her main facial features, and her hair was off her shoulders and elaborately braided to one side of her head.

Whilst Emma appeared radiant in what she was wearing, she was experiencing inner turmoil. She had found David not the most exciting company, and whilst he was easy enough to talk to, she just considered him a good friend.

She wanted to find and talk to Archie Malcolm and David had mentioned in the pub the previous day that he was to be at the ball. She needed to find out more about him. Emma had only played hockey occasionally with Archie and chatted to him in passing at other student's houses, so they had had a limited friendship.

He always came across as a slightly closed book, but that was what was so intriguing about him. He was so polite and always asked her how she was doing and what she was up to. What about him? She told David that she needed to pop to the ladies and they arranged to meet each other at the casino in ten minutes.

The Student Union was busy now and any moving about was a slow process. There was a photographer set up to snap away at the various groups and many of the teams were having photographs together, a serious one and others that should never be printed, let alone sold.

David pushed past a few of his colleagues to reach the gents. He went in and headed for the fourth cubical in the corner. He locked the door and tapped his foot on the ground discreetly twice. The man in the neighbouring cubical slid a large packet of a white substance under the partitioning. This had already been split into small sachets. David immediately placed the packet in the top of the toilet cistern whilst the man in the neighbouring cubicle whispered through to David, "I'll be back for our controller's cut tomorrow night, don't be late,"

David just said, "Thanks, Betts," before he heard the 'Out of Order' sticker being applied to his fourth cubicle door.

CHAPTER 59

Archie flew in mid-air as the bungee cord pulled him with all its might back where he had stood moments before.

In line with the two other lads who were running down the alleys to his left and right he had confidently eyed up his inflated alleyway corridor. Archie had directly faced the cowboy hat which was just out of reach. It was only ten metres from his grasp. He had thought it would have been easy, but now he was not so sure. A different approach was required.

Archie crouched low. He would grab the cowboy hat if it was the last item on earth that required saving. In itself it was not a special hat. Made of a standard, dark-brown leather with a woven light and dark brown edging it did not shout out, but it was what the hat represented.

Archie took a deep intake of breath, put his weight forward and his legs were suddenly working overtime, as if he had been put in an ever faster spinning, hamster wheel. The blown up inflatable structure had not provided much grip. Archie had realised that to make any progress up the aisle he had needed to remove his socks so that he was bare footed. The once civilized naval officer and PhD student was nearing the cowboy hat like a ferocious pit-bull.

Archie was serious. He would not be denied his prize. He felt the pull of the elastic bungee cord around his waist and it was beginning to strain against the direction that Archie was taking. His legs were now working even faster, he felt the heat of his exertion all over him; from his forehead to his arms and legs and around the cord of the bungee line which was desperately seeking to bring him back to the mother ship of the start-line.

Archie dived forward using the momentum he had built up and flew through the air to land a couple of metres further forward and within grasp of the cowboy hat. He outstretched his hand and reached with all his might with his fingers. His arm felt as though it was going to dislocate, such was the force with which he stretched himself out.

The brown leather cowboy hat remained out of reach. The expression on Archie's face was comical. He really could not believe it. The bungee cord now had Archie in its power. There was no running away from the elastic bouncing him back whence he had come. There were quite a few giggles as Archie flew backwards through the air, away from the prized cowboy hat and back to his starting position. He landed in a heap on the ground of his inflatable corridor. He no longer presented the dapper image he had just a few moments ago, as Lieutenant Archie Malcolm in his military pose, oozing sophistication.

Never to be outdone, Archie sprung to his feet. He had been within a hair's breath, and maybe, maybe if he just moved the waist harness of the bungee a little further down and stretched a little more, the prize would be his.

His legs whirled even faster than before, his slim pit-bull pose attacking every inch of the blown up inflatable corridor. The onlookers changed their tune and willed him on. There was the start of a handclap which began to pick up pace. Archie seized the moment. He felt his audience willing him on and this spurred him to work even harder. Down the inflatable corridor he went, perspiring even harder, launching himself for the hat with such force that it seemed to flinch on its pedestal.

Archie stretched his fingers to their full extent and brushed the leather material. He was not letting this one escape. He reached up with his other arm. The hat was in the grip of his hand. He was victorious. His admirers began to clap. The cowboy hat had found its way to his head. He was asked to choose a card from the five in the man's hand.

Archie was thinking that he had never won anything in his life. The last few moments had changed all of that. He was being hoisted against his will onto many of the students' shoulders. He was still attempting to draw the card. Lifting it up to his eyes he read:

"You have won a romantic evening for two at Yves restaurant, Cropston, Nr. Winchester, Hampshire. This card entitles the bearer to £200 worth of spending for a wonderful, memorable occasion."

Wow, what an evening that will be, thought Archie. He knew exactly who he wanted to spend it with.

CHAPTER 60

Emma had spied Archie on her return from the ladies room. He had been running vigorously to grab the cowboy hat. She was impressed with the sense of fun about him, as well as his fine figure. Athletically throwing himself for the prize, he just did not give up and the commitment to the task was remarkable. She made herself part of the handclap, and clapped louder and louder until he was victorious.

Archie was being carried now by a hoard of spectators and had ripped open the card upon which was written his prize. His face lit up with glee and Emma could not help herself from thinking that it made him more attractive, pronouncing his slight dimples and crinkling his forehead above the eyebrows.

Emma walked round to find David at the casino table. David seemed to be gambling away as much money as he could. It certainly was not going his way as Emma heard him curse quietly and then more obviously; loud enough for the dealer and his fellow gamblers to raise their heads and sigh or tut, or even appear to show expressions of sympathy. David was having horrendous luck. Where was all his money coming from? Emma urged David to stop throwing his money away as he appeared to have little left. David ignored her protestations. He was in his own little world and oblivious to what was going on around him.

Previously bored, and now irritated by being ignored, Emma went to find Archie. Archie, oh... she needed some courage and had to go to the bar first.

Whilst at the bar Emma noticed that David had walked through the union to the outside area, presumably for some fresh air. She would catch up with her date later, for now there were more important people to be with.

Archie Malcolm had seen Emma head for the bar as he was being put down onto terra firma. She was looking lovely and he so needed to speak to her. This was just his moment and no-one was going to stop him.

"I'm buying," he shouted to the barman from a few metres away, tapping Emma on the far shoulder so that she turned her head in the wrong direction. He nodded a pint of the local to be added to the large glass of wine that Emma was drinking. She turned the right way, gazing deeply into his eyes and smiled,

"I've been wanting to talk to you," she started…

It was difficult for Archie to hear as the music was coming alive and everyone seemed to have headed over to the large student bar adjacent to the dance floor. The rodeo bull, the casino and the inflatable alleyways had come to an end so all the people who had been energetically part of the activities or gambling their small fortunes away were now heading for drinks.

"Same here," Archie shouted back. "Can we go outside?" He pointed at his ears as he really could not hear and grabbed one of her hands and led her outside. Her hand was warm, and a tingly sensation rose up the whole of his arm. It felt good.

The cool air was in stark contrast to the heat of the union and as Emma was only wearing her purple shift, she suddenly appeared a little cold.

Archie pointed to his prize and read the words aloud again to Emma.

"Emma, I want you to be my dinner date for the evening. Can I take you to the restaurant?"

"I would love to go with you," Emma responded without hesitation.

Emma quickly thought of her time in the Alps, and apart from the scary night on the mountain in a survival bag, it had been a wonderful break with her family. She also now thought of the voice in the night, she was sure it had been Archie Malcolm. She innocently asked what he had been up to over the last couple of weeks as she had not seen him around the campus or any of the usual student haunts.

Archie sensed the alarm bells and skillfully avoided the question, referring to the wonderful walks he had had along the seafront, how his ringing was going, and his plans to pop over to the Isle of Wight in the near future.

Meanwhile, a white van had reversed into the rear car park of the Student Union and stopped, with its engine still running, five metres away from where Archie and Emma were standing. The driver's door swung open and a man in a skull cap got out and opened up the rear doors.

David appeared from nowhere and went to speak to the man. The rear doors opened again to briefly reveal packages. All were neatly and individually wrapped. The rusty old doors were slammed closed. Archie was intrigued and distracted. He hugged Emma so that she was facing the Student Union building and he was hidden by this beautiful girl, who was definitely hugging him back. The skullcap man went back to the driver's door and there was something very familiar about him.

The muscular frame and the movement were unique and very memorable. Skullcap man was now in the van and revving the engine. It was Betts. Archie finally clicked and belatedly glared at the van as it took off out of the back of the Student Union car park.

CHAPTER 61

Betts made his exit in the white Ford Transit van that he had picked up from the self-hire van garage on the approach road into Portsmouth.

Fidgeting in his driver's seat and very aware of the value of the goods contained in the rear of his vehicle, he headed to the rendezvous with Natalia, the leader of the South American supply operation. Together they would meet the UK controller. The time had come. It sent shivers down his spine.

Having pointed a loaded pistol at the pilot of the helicopter back in the Alpine wilderness in order to facilitate his escape from the clutches of Lieutenant Archie Malcolm's naval squad, Betts needed to ensure that he remained invisible until the end of his own operation.

He only received his entire fee when the crack team set up to hunt them all down was called off. Having disposed of Kevin, James and Nick, he was determined to do what was required to receive the remainder of his money.

The roads were a little icy at this time of night, the weather having been cold over the last few days. It was only a short hop to the small freighter terminal but Betts wanted to ensure that he did not have a tail. He therefore wove the van around the edge of Southsea from the Student Union, carrying out a quick loop into the cobbled streets of Old Portsmouth.

If there was anyone following him, they would not be able to hide away from this manoeuvre. A tail would still have to know which direction he was taking, and have to show himself somewhere within the small cobbled streets of the Old Town. All appeared quiet and Betts relaxed a little.

He turned onto the main dock road which led to the temporarily constructed freighter port. He could not shake off his excitement. It was truly momentous for him. An ordinary Navy man who had been dedicated to his country and his current employers, the Royal Navy, but now to have woken up to an alternative and much larger source of income. Yes, few would be prepared to have carried out what he had done. Murder, yes, he would always have to live with that, but then his morals had left him many moons ago.

Single for most of his adult life, Betts had travelled the world, visiting most of the great sea faring ports and sampling everything that they had to offer. Whilst being single, it did not mean that he had not enjoyed the company of the fairer sex. His life on board meant that he had plenty of time to speculate over his next conquest. Too much time, it had turned out. His appetite for sex had become an obsession, a compulsion to sow his wild oats across the globe, and his own black book grew and grew until he was rarely concentrating on the real work that he undertook.

Even now, his mind wandered back to the much talked about Natalia. She was a phenomenon. Betts had been on a frigate many years ago that had called in at Lima, Peru. He had been given shore leave and what an episode it had been. He vividly recalled the excitement of the bars and nightlife in this South American capital. He also remembered every moment because, in one of the seedier centrally located bars, he had been introduced to the Morales brothers. He had met these young wolves and kept up with their drinking. They had been impressed.

For Betts, it was a routine evening away from work until they asked him for a favour. The favour had seemed fairly innocent and easy at the time. It was to smuggle some of their goods back to the UK and pass them on to be sold at a profit. The Morales gave him the contact to meet up with and to deliver the necessary cut into the Morales bank account.

Over the years, the Morales had helped to keep Petty Officer Betts going, and fuel his expensive taste for women. That one occasion he had met the Morales brothers, had been the only time. The Morales had been careful to distance themselves and contact was always made thereafter using their chain system.

He had dreamt and fantasised about the legendary Natalia, and at last he was to be meeting her. His heart skipped a beat and he instinctively put his right foot further down on the accelerator.

CHAPTER 62

Natalia gazed at the city of Portsmouth from the bridge of the freighter. The light breeze rustled wisps of her dark hair across her face. She tucked them behind her right ear and pulled down her warm hat so it entirely covered the back of her head.

The Captain had sensed that she needed support after her ordeal. He could not comprehend the thought of losing two brothers. It was enough to make anyone feel compassionate for the sole sibling remaining.

Captain Sharkey had been hugely sympathetic. Normally brimming with life, enthusiasm and extremely gregarious, the effect of the presumed loss of life on his ship had had a profound impact. The Captain had treated Natalia as a daughter. Like all of his family members and crew, he cared for Natalia as best he could. In a not dissimilar fashion to the Morales way, the Captain tried to help Natalia come to terms with her immediate shock over the first forty-eight hours of her loss. He saw to her meals, her drinks and that she had a comfortable cabin to sleep in. Her own cabin had been affected by the fire so it was important that she moved and took up quarters near the Captain's cabin.

Natalia's mind had been a blur. Her thoughts were confused. She had needed space over the last couple of days since the incident to work out how she was to cope with the recent course of events. It would take her much longer to come to terms with what had happened, but the immediate priorities gave her a focus.

Yes, her mind was able to concentrate on the here and now. She would try and push the recent events to the back of her mind and concentrate on the moment. It was worth channelling her remaining energies to justify all the planning and preparation that had gone before. In just another twenty-four hours all the supply would be out in the market place and she could start recouping the monies that she and her family were due.

Potentially, they would make thousands of pounds sterling, hundreds of thousands, perhaps much more than that. Certain suppliers and distributors did have to be paid and without her brothers' strong arm support, Natalia reflected that they might have to be paid in full. This was worrying. There had to be a way around it. There was never enough cash in the pot for everyone. If Natalia was to succeed then this had to be at the expense of others.

Thinking about the next few hours was crucial. She selected her outfit and read up on Betts, their man on the inside who had kept the UK authorities at bay. He had done well so far, but nothing lasted forever, did it? Her packages needed to be followed and kept tabs on, both the car and the other smaller goods. Betts would play his part and allow the final distribution meeting to take place.

CHAPTER 63

Natalia had wanted to have immediate control of Betts's mind and body. To do so, she had dressed appropriately. She knew about his past and the wanderings of this man and she would lure him where she wanted him to follow.

The Spanish in Natalia had been creative with her hair braided. It had also been seductive. She hid the fact that she was not wearing just a simple sweater from the crew and Captain by her long woollen dark coat. This kept her warm and gave her an air of anonymity.

The freighter gently touched the wooden mooring posts and the crew lowered the mooring lines to the waiting dockside workers. As the boat was secured, arrangements were quickly being made for the cranes to start unloading the crates in the hold and for any deck cargo to be separately swung to shore using the freighter's smaller hoists.

The boat became a sea of life, with the cranes swinging back and forth. Urgent instructions were being given to low loaders on the shore if certain sea crates needed moving, and the customs officials were already taking an interest in a number of the crates as it was clear that the freighter had travelled directly from Lima, which was rare.

Natalia trod carefully down the gangplank in her sensible trainers and jogging bottoms. These were her first footsteps on the United Kingdom's rich soil and she enjoyed practising her accented English phrases as she entered the passenger customs area. Her documents were checked without comment and she proceeded to the ladies room.

It was a different, stunning lady that left the same room

twenty minutes later, appearing immaculate and beautiful and, well, breathtaking. She had make-up that accented her strong Spanish face with off-red rouge on the lips and light mascara hidden behind the designer sunglasses. The figure hugging black top accented her natural curves and highlighted the medium sized pearls that sat above the rise and fall of her breasts.

Natalia was proud of her legs and showed them off to full effect. The stockings would be saved for Betts's touch if she really had to go that far. The high heels kept her on tip-toe and accented and extenuated the shape of her athletic lower limbs, which seemed to have been exaggerated by the belt-sized skirt.

The black, tightly fitted micro-skirt was short. Short enough for the person wearing it to keep pulling it down around the edges, to immediately cross their legs whenever sitting and to appear to be brushing crumbs or dust off the front when in reality the wearer had realised that she had gone too far and was not wearing enough material.

Natalia, however, was in a position of power. She felt in control. She soaked up and absorbed the mainly male glances of lust, the female glances of spite and jealousy, and confidently stepped out into the passenger pick-up point.

There was the man in his rusty van; waiting like a puppy dog. He was late middle-age, and still in good physical shape, although past his prime. The hair was fighting the brown-grey war and he had a very determined look on his face, but she could see that he knew of her reputation and would do what she said. It had to be Betts.

Natalia walked straight towards him and Betts had to recover from his natural male desire to look at anything except this beautiful Spanish woman's face. He stared at Natalia and gazed directly into her hard eyes. He immediately came to the conclusion that she had experienced much in her life and like himself, had had to confront tough issues head on. They were kindred spirits, he thought. Betts would stop at nothing and do whatever it would take to know this lady thoroughly.

Having had years of experience, Betts pulled out the charm. He scurried round to the passenger door and opened it for her. He paused for the extra second to enable her to adjust her skirt to hoist herself into the seat.

Driving to the top hotel in the area where Natalia was staying her first night, Betts missed the gear stick and accidentally stroked Natalia's stockinged thigh. She just smiled as though she had not noticed. Betts was not aware of the irritation that lay just behind her outward mask.

Natalia asked just one question on the journey, "Is my consignment safe, Betts?"

"Yes it is, Senorita Morales," Betts replied.

CHAPTER 64

David had discussed the importance of their consignment with Betts. They stood side by side as links in the long Morales chain. It was an interlocking relationship and relied on both the men trusting each other, for this marriage of convenience allowed the respective partners to make money. They certainly benefited from the efficiencies, and conversely suffered from the inefficiencies, of each other.

Betts had been pumped full of adrenalin at setting off to meet Natalia, and David was excited for him. Unable to concentrate whilst gambling within the Student Union, the pocket money that he had lost would soon be replaced by a proper wage; a wage that he had earned through his hard work, he reminded himself.

It had taken years for him to become the main dealer of cocaine in Portsmouth. His clients respected him. They relied on the quality and regularity of his supply and knew they needed to pay up in full, otherwise they would be at risk of not seeing him again.

Turning away from Betts' van which was quickly exiting the rear car park of the Student Union, David was in the mood for a few drinks. He strode towards the bar and sat himself on one of the free upright stools.

"Two lagers, please," he shouted at Corinne serving behind the bar.

There was only the one of him, but he wanted to make a quick start. He had other matters to attend to. It had been pushed to the back of his mind what was happening with his date for the evening. His concentration had been on the cocaine supply for the evening in the Student Union to ensure his few hundred pounds during the course of the ball. He had completely lost track of Emma.

In focusing on the quick encounter and send off for Betts, his other half had wandered off. David was sure that he had last been with her by the casino tables, but they were closed now. All who had been on the bucking bronco, or on the blow up bungee corridors or at the casino, were now in the main bar area and the various sitting areas that led off.

David appeared pained. This had been a chance to progress his personal life with the most beautiful girl at the university and yet his mind had been elsewhere. He never knew when to stop. He could not help himself. Had Emma been his chance to escape? Could he convince his own soul that he really had been able to remove himself from the mess that he was in?

He could not see her anywhere. He shouted at Corinne for another couple of lagers and slouched back against the edge of the bar, the stool which he had perched on earlier had now been taken and his mood was worsening. The couple next to him were all over each other and this just made matters worse. He gazed in the other direction and took in the small happy crowds of team players, their housemates and some of the friends becoming very close friends.

He downed the first pint of the new round, picked up the second and walked around the whole of the bar area and the seating areas off it in a similar fashion to a lost sheep. He had to leave. He had created his own personal mess and he would be the one to pull himself out of his current situation. He would show Emma that he was not a lost cause; his future wealth would guarantee admiration from others and that they would look up to him. He would not be a worthless individual. Money would ensure others loved him.

David left the union by the front main entrance and

walked out past the bouncer on the gate. Next to him were students who had not pre-bought a ticket, queuing outside to join in the party. The ball was now just beginning to liven up, with the music blaring out its regular beats into the neighbouring streets.

David walked along the familiar roads across town. They eventually led him to the back of St. Mary's Church in the northern part of the island. The church was never properly lit up, and suffered from vandalism. There was a new cracked window just to the side of the entrance and a temporary piece of plywood had been propped up on the inside of the building.

The height of the historic architecture cast long shadows in the moonlit evening and the air was still. Nobody was about and David was an unnoticed, solitary figure. He hugged the dark buttresses of the tower and found the pathway that signalled the direction his footsteps needed to take.

Ensuring that no-one was behind him, David opened the manhole cover set low in the pathway and descended the shiny new loft-ladder that he had installed especially.

He shone his torch in the gloom and found the wooden door padlock. Turning his standard key released the bolt, and David walked through to the room beyond.

Huddled in their respective beds under the large grey blankets was a middle aged woman in the larger adult sized bed and a young teenage girl in the smaller bed adjacent. The torchlight picked out the links of the chains that led to the right ankles of each of the prisoners. The skin had chafed slightly on both the mother and daughter where the chain had resisted their movement around the room. David reflected that the pair had behaved themselves throughout their ordeal. Even he was aware that the two of them had been insurance for the Woodcutter's actions, whoever the Woodcutter was.

CHAPTER 65

David turned off his torch and sat in the wooden chair facing the two beds. In the partial light his eyes became accustomed to the shape of the room.

The feet of the adult bed had been screwed down into the wooden floor that lay in the far corner, with the headboard resting against the breeze block wall. Adjacent to it was the smaller bed, in which the daughter now lay. This bed was naturally heavier and difficult for David to move on his own, let alone a teenage girl or her mother.

There was a single bulb close to where he was sitting but the mother and daughter knew better than to put the light on outside of daytime hours. How did they know that it was daytime if they were cramped into a one-bedroom temporary prison? David had installed a large face clock so that they would keep to his nine until four rule. With the seasons changing, the natural light crept into the room before and after their day and ensured there was another hour in which to absorb their horrific surroundings.

The ladies were tethered to the bed frames by means of the chains which led to their ankles. The number of links meant that they could freely stand and walk an arc within a couple of metres from the main wooden door to use the chamber pot which was on the floor in the opposite corner of this underground cellar.

All had become used to their mind-numbing routines. David had attempted to build-up a library for his captives and collect the various magazines which they requested. As a television or video had been out of the question he had borrowed a portable DVD player and provided films that had been subtitled.

The situation had become out of his control. Originally believing that he just had to ensure that the mother and daughter were to be kept safe for a couple of nights, ("It's for their own good you know," the controller had said), the current scenario had escalated beyond his worst fears.

The couple of days had drawn into a week, the week into a few weeks and now the mother and daughter had been held captive against their will for over two months. The situation had to end and it had to end soon.

The predicted, and actual, arrival of the freighter had led David to believe that the end was in sight. He could feel it, sniff it and taste it. The way in which other people were acting signified that there would be a defined sense of closure to this episode in his life. Perhaps then he could leave this messy juncture and stop hiding his horrible secret world that was required for his get rich quick plan.

David began to cry. A quiet, sobbing, sniffling sound that was not quite a weeping but all his pent up emotion over the years seemed to escalate into these long drawn out gentle sobs. He had nobody to comfort him. David, the orphan, felt alone and isolated in the world. He had gone down a route of his choosing and it was leading him to destruction. He had to get out but how?

CHAPTER 66

Emma felt good, and it was not only Emma who was thinking this. Archie was absorbing her breath on his neck. Drinking in her body, her curves, her warmth. She felt cosy. She fitted into him. She helped to make him feel complete.

At the same moment, as the van had rapidly escaped from the Student Union car park with his former team mate, the murderer Betts behind the wheel, stirred enormous emotion within him.

After being taken off the mission by Commander Edgar Bennett, Malcolm had sought to push the whole episode in the Alps from his mind. Try as he might, he was unable to hide and temper his feelings from Emma. She asked him what was wrong. Archie shrugged. He could not put into words what was building up inside him. Instead, Archie remained aloof and stated that he could not explain but that it was nothing to do with her.

Archie suggested they go inside out of the cold. Emma had cooled down so immediately agreed.

"I could do with a hot drink, Archie, as well as a hot man!"

Archie was taken aback. Here was this beautiful, gorgeous, lovely girl who had just jokingly complimented him and was clearly enjoying his company.

He chuckled "I don't know about the last bit, but let's get out of here; I'll show you where I live." He hastily added, "There's no compulsion to come in but I do have a very comfortable sofa, so you can have my bedroom and I'll sleep in the lounge."

"OK, you've twisted my arm," laughed Emma.

Archie and Emma walked hand in hand down to the Hard and continued past the seafront and the Portsmouth fortifications to the entrance of Archie's block of flats. Archie was on a high. The alcohol he had consumed gave him a rosy glow, but the main reason for his high spirits was Emma. Their early relationship seemed to be blossoming. Yes, he wanted to know her more in every way, but he did not want to lose her or rush becoming acquainted with her. By understanding her and knowing her properly, he would treasure the unravelling of this special girl.

Once in his flat, Archie made them both hot chocolates and Emma remained shy and observant and told Archie how she had ended up studying geography at Portsmouth University. The darkness of the night could not hide the glinting masts of the yachts moored up in Haslar Marina, their hulls quietly floating on the opposite side of the Portsmouth Harbour entrance.

Whilst enjoying the coastal location of Portsmouth, Emma was not a great seafarer. Time spent in her youth with her family crossing the Channel on one of the many ferries had always caused her to react to the up and down motion of the waves and tides. Despite attempting different tactics of eating or not eating prior to the crossings, taking sea sickness pills and seeking the fresh-air of the deck, the travelling by boat element of those holidays had never been much fun. Archie was amused that she always felt seasick on the water that they were both gazing at.

Emma made a point of not going on boats anymore, in her holiday time or otherwise. She was in her element jogging along the sea-front on her weekly run to Eastney and back. The wind never seemed to be completely calm and the number of watercraft off the shore always meant that the view across to the Isle of Wight was filled with activity and interest. Passing Southsea Pier there would be the amusements, candy floss and rock sellers. The fish and chip shops would come next before watching the putters on the seafront golf course. She enjoyed these times, not having to worry about her coursework or the next assignment as she was taking in the comings and goings of the sea-craft and the seafront, and the distance would fly under her running shoes.

As Emma opened up, Archie was impressed by her get up and go. It matched his. Archie and Emma had much in common and this was especially apparent when she turned to winter sports. When Emma told Archie of her recent family holiday and how she and her two brothers had come to be within an orange winter survival bag on the side of the mountain below the Glacier de Bellecote, Archie did not know where to put himself or how to respond. He did what he knew best, he listened. He took in every word, the shape of her lips, the truthful and open eyes, the warmth and love for her family, the fighting spirit.

Emma was absorbing this wonderful man concentrating immensely on her every word. She knew there was more, and she had been waiting to find a moment to understand fully what had happened that night.

"You were there, Archie, weren't you?"

It was not a rhetorical question and Emma continued to wait for a response. Archie just remained calm and attempted to mask his face. It had been such a wonderful evening. Everything had been perfect and now this. What was he to say? Did he compromise his position for the girl that he had fallen madly in love with? Was it love? Was that really what he felt? He had never had emotions like this about anybody before. Could he trust her?

"I think we both need another hot chocolate, Emma," Archie began hesitantly and then picked up his voice. "Or perhaps we should have something a little stronger. There's been much that I've wanted to say to you and seeing that I'm away from it all and I trust you, Emma, let me share with you what I've been doing over the last nine months."

CHAPTER 67

Archie tasted the warmth of the hot chocolate and began his tale. The effect of what he had said before, with the sound of obvious emotion in his voice, meant they both devoured the couple of extra gulps of brandy that Archie poured unsteadily into their drinks.

Emma was rapt in attention. Archie began with his role in the armed forces as well as his PhD student studying. Emma was impressed that Archie had been identified as having exceptional qualities by the Royal Navy, but by no means surprised. A team player, a gregarious and intelligent character, his reports had read. He blushed with embarrassment for the regular updates had also stated: leadership potential, someone whom you respected for his wisdom and ability to see things through. This is what Archie was, what he stood for. It was all very clear to Emma.

Archie had been given small leadership tasks at first and had built up a team of trusted individuals. Petty Officer Betts had always been on the edge of the trusted team, sometimes included, sometimes not.

The shooting test seemed many months ago now, almost approaching three quarters of a year, but he had seen part of the man's real character. Their mission to the Alps had been decided and they all set out to become familiar with the lay of the land, to increase their fitness, and develop their winter training skills. Kevin had been out in the field becoming adept at communications and Jackie and Jo had spent hours pouring over the reconnaissance pictures of the remote Alpine valley and its surrounds, complete with the planned landing site.

Emma took a quick swig of her hot chocolate whilst gazing continuously at Archie. She needed to read his body language, to be sure that she could trust him. She did not want to miss a detail and she knew the important part was coming up.

Archie re-told how the team had skydived to just below the Glacier de Bellecote and had been off target on the landing; so off target that they had ended up gathered to the side of the main bulk of the dome of the imposing rocky outcrop. In the growing light of dawn, it had been confusing to see what appeared to be a bright orange winter survival bag.

Indeed, in checking the contents there had been the three young adults, Emma and two young men, all perishing cold. Archie told Emma of his anguish at the time; how he had eventually contacted the French rescue teams, ensured that they had enough food, water and an extra blanket and attempted to push Joseph back inside. Archie had been concerned that Joseph might have vague recollections of the incident.

Emma confirmed to Archie that these were her brothers, how she had felt at the time and after having been rescued, that she could not work out why she had Archie Malcolm's voice in her head.

Archie pulled Emma back into his story with the deaths of Kevin, who had appeared to parachute off the mountain and, soon after, of James and Nick. He elaborated on the circumstances, confirming that the men had died whilst attempting to stop the Woodcutter from escaping in his micro-light from the discreet wooden chalet, and Betts from escaping in the team's helicopter transport. His teammates' deaths would not be in vain.

Emma took in the unusual fiery emotion of this man to whom she was completely warming. It may have been four in the morning on this Sunday in the turn of spring, but that was the first time she had glanced at the clock since going to the ball with David the previous evening. Where was David now? She did not really care. She wanted to be here with Archie. Archie's issues were hers. How could she help him? How could Archie avenge the deaths of his colleagues when he had been taken off the mission?

Archie pulled himself out of his seat and walked over to the sliding doors leading onto the wooden balcony. He turned the black handle and the cool breeze rushed into the flat. It seemed to bring both of them into the immediate present and intimacy of their surroundings. Emma rose to join Archie and they stepped out onto the balcony into the pre-dawn.

Emma was still in her beautiful purple dress and her purple neck band had loosened. Archie untied it and kissed Emma gently where, moments before, it had covered her skin. She reacted by drawing him close to her and she kissed him back lightly on the lips.

Archie found Emma's gentle kiss exquisite, so beautiful that this moment had to be treasured. It took all his will to lead Emma to his bed, to kiss her softly on the cheek and then return to his own sofa bed. The burning desire would have to wait.

The address that Nick had found in the basement of the chalet in the Alps was heavy in Archie's pocket, having lain there far too long. Emma had reignited his passions, both emotionally for her and for his former team mates. He was now more determined than ever to avenge the deaths of his colleagues.

CHAPTER 68

The Tower Captain had woken early as the house martins were noisy this morning. The birds were making their nest on this beautiful spring day just metres from where his head had been lying on the down filled pillows. Even with a single pane of glass set into this beautiful Tudor home, their cheeps and chirps cut through the envelope of the property into the bedroom.

Their calls stirred the late middle aged man to life. Mavis was still sleeping next to him as he rolled out of bed. He reached for his dressing gown and padded downstairs, ducking under a couple of oak beams. Whilst a beautiful property, it had a number of impractical characteristics, one of which was the height under the sturdy oak beams at first floor level.

The Tower Captain filled up the kettle and made sure it would soon be bubbling away. He checked on the home-made bread that his wife had prepared the previous evening. The smell of the bread was still in the air and he lingered before shuffling over to the downstairs closet.

So as not to disturb his wife when he was back at home from his weekly consultancy role in the city, he had had the closet installed near the back of the house. In addition to holding his gun cabinet, always kept under lock and key, there were his basic outdoor clothes and a clean set of undergarments.

The Tower Captain dressed and put on his Wellington boots and Barbour jacket. Closing the back door as quietly as possible, he walked along the gravel path to the small outhouses a hundred metres away from the main house. It really was a beautiful spring morning, he thought. It was going to be an exceptional day and this was just the start he needed. The bulbs were in full flower. He had seen the end of the crocuses and the snowdrops and it was now the turn of the mighty daffodils and tulips. His garden, though more realistically described as an estate, was starting to come into life.

He was reminded of his conversation with a fellow consultant in the city earlier in the week.

"Spring in the air," the consultant had exclaimed, as the warmth and smells of spring had even pervaded the heart of the capital.

The Tower Captain had responded, "Spring in the air yourself!" Once he had caught on, both of the city workers had chuckled for quite a while there after.

Reaching the outhouses and their surrounding yard, he peered into the first enclosure. *Pinkie* and *Perkie*, his two six month old black Berkshire pigs shuffled back towards him. They were looking very well indeed. Having created a large mound of earth immediately outside of their sty, their noses, acting like very efficient shovels, were working the ground over, adjacent to the sty itself. A treat to watch, he could not believe the pigs were approaching six months. Their standard of living had allowed them to put on a good amount of weight and hoover up scraps, potatoes and everything else that they were given.

The Tower Captain walked into the small outbuilding opposite, which contained his small flock. He checked that the feeders and the water containers were working properly and full and that his hens and cockerel were well. Most importantly, he went to the nesting areas where he removed half a dozen eggs and smiled at the beauty of it all.

Lastly, he completed his round by walking over to the

paddock fences. He reflected that he had erected these fences with his bare hands. What a feat that had been! Gazing over the Hampshire countryside had helped to make it all worthwhile. His alpacas and llamas stayed a respectful distance away. These animals enjoyed their own space and, still being fairly new to the Tower Captain, he was enjoying gaining an understanding of their ways.

As this was a special day, the Tower Captain wanted to check on the space that he had created in the garaging next to the outhouses. With a spring in his step, he quickly opened up the triple doors and lovingly stared at his restored MGB with original metallic spokes and beautiful, dark brown interior trim. He had always been a fan of classic cars, but for his new addition it was not just going to be about the car now, was it?

Turning towards his beautiful home with its higgledy piggledy exterior, he removed the Sunday paper from the jet black post box by the dark wooden entrance gates and proceeded back to the rear entrance.

Checking the kettle had boiled, he poured the three mugs of tea, knocking on Monica's door to let her know that Daddy had made her weekend early morning cuppa.

The Tower Captain was proud of his daughter Monica. Not naturally into reading or writing, she had found school and studies difficult. As her father, the Tower Captain had been unsure where her future lay. When he had first moved into his alternative businesses he had soon realised the value of trust. His consultancy role in the city which he had developed over the years, had always been an excellent cover.

Naturally a cautious person leaving nothing to chance, the Tower Captain was aware that these attributes had served him well. His own parents had always said "Leave no stone unturned," or "Go the extra mile." The Tower Captain also believed that if you wanted something badly enough, or cared about the quality of the output of your work, then it was always worth doing it to the best of your ability.

The Tower Captain's activities were particularly sensitive; he needed to share the details with as few people as practically possible. Monica was one of those people. Whilst perhaps appearing outwardly dippy, her father knew that he could trust her implicitly. The unassuming exterior was one of her strengths as this ensured that those around Monica relaxed in her company, trusted her, and more importantly, shared their thoughts and what was going on in their lives.

The Tower Captain, his wife Mavis and their daughter Monica were all going into the centre of Portsmouth today. Each of them made their way through boiled eggs and dippers and a further piece of toast, with freshly made marmalade.

"Wonderful fresh bread and marmalade," the Tower Captain said to his wife. Mavis confirmed agreement and that she thought the brown worked much better with the seed mix added. Monica made it clear that they should all keep moving and grabbed her black leather jacket. The Tower Captain considered it too small as it rose up and showed her midriff, but that was all the rage apparently.

The family party locked up the main house and headed over to the outbuildings. The Tower Captain revved up the large Audi and they were on their way, sweeping along the drive of the estate, the house screened by the extensive landscaping. Out into the rolling Hampshire countryside, the car passed along the narrow rural lanes which would meet up with the M27 to take them into the heart of the City of Portsmouth.

The Tower Captain dropped Monica off discreetly at the top end of the pedestrianised high street. She had some weekend shopping to do and was required to undertake some overtime at the naval base in the afternoon. In view of her efficiency, Commander Edgar Bennett had ensured that Monica now fulfilled the role of his personal assistant. It was an invaluable role for Monica and for her family, to have someone on the inside, and of course outwardly for the Commander as he believed that she was efficiently fulfilling all of her duties and had no suspicions.

The Tower Captain and Mavis continued onto the cobbled streets of Old Portsmouth and parked the large vehicle on one of the recently metered side streets. The Cathedral stood out brightly ahead, the twin towers of the western façade contrasting with the pale blue of the sky. The Tower Captain and Mavis walked round to the gated side entrance and up the wide, internal, stone steps. Walking past the organ, Mavis paused briefly to catch her breath and turned to look out over the main body of the Cathedral with all of the wooden chairs for the congregation below.

The Tower Captain unlocked the small wooden door that led up to the ringing chamber and they both proceeded up the small flight of indented, stone steps that wound round to the right. This layout, the Tower Captain thought, had stemmed from the right handed defender coming down the stairs needing the sword arm advantage in the event of a siege.

Opening up the ringing chamber door, the Tower Captain quickly carried out his initial duties. He took the clock chimes off. He wound the clock using the long metal handle for leverage. He lowered the pulley holding all of the ringing ropes and started to tie up all of the ropes individually so that their ends were not loose on the polished wooden floor.

He checked that the necessary arrangements were in place next door to the ringing chamber, and then went up the oak ladder into the belfry. His tool kit lay to the side of the tenor bell and it only took him five minutes to complete his task.

It was a shame that it had come to this. The lad had come too close to spoiling it all and he had to be removed. The

Tower Captain's assistants had requested help after the episode in the Alps. Lieutenant Archie Malcolm had to be dispatched, and the Tower Captain needed to play his part. If you are going to do something, do it well.

CHAPTER 69

Natalia was in a rush to escape from her hotel room. Yes, it was by far the best hotel she had ever stayed in. Yes, it had panoramic views of the Solent, a helpful concierge, and all her needs had been catered for. What it could not do, though, was reunite Natalia with her brothers or with her treasured cargo.

She was attempting to squeeze the last of her expensive clothes into her case. It still would not close. She sat on it and then needed to put all of her weight above the opening clasps. At last, the case locks joined with the clasps and clicked into place.

All she could think about was the contents of the classic car and the distribution of the other packages across the UK. Would it all go smoothly? Would there be any issues with the authorities? She was ready to do what she could to stamp her way, the Morales way, on the whole of the UK operation. She was sure that monies which were illegitimately the Morales' were being siphoned off by the local dealers and the main controller overseeing this local network.

She would skip breakfast and go for a walk across the Common, which she had spied from her seafront suite. She needed to clear her mind, and be ready for her meeting with the local operatives.

The hotel concierge nodded at her as she skipped out of the main front door on this fresh spring morning. She smelt the salt in the breeze and was impressed by the real green of the Common; a far cry from the natural browns of her native Peru.

It was a short walk that would take her to the embankment of the seafront itself, with the road and promenade lying in front of the Southsea War Memorial. This was just what she needed. Feeling properly revitalised, after a deeper than normal sleep, she was ready to do battle. She could work out who she could trust and who would help take their family fortune further, and who just needed to be removed and eliminated.

It was an easy, looped walk back to the hotel where she was to meet Betts, who had refused to let her know where the meeting was being held. It was a matter of the utmost secrecy even from her, and this ensured that there were no unnecessary leaks. Betts had reluctantly left her the previous evening, and had been sure to take in the whole aura of Natalia, prior to departing for his separate digs, located only a couple of streets away from the Common, close to Southsea Shopping Centre.

Betts had arranged to meet Natalia at 9am. He was visibly disappointed to see her wearing a smart, practical, trouser suit and Betts himself was, unusually attired in good quality clothes. His ensemble consisted of a fresh pair of jeans, a smart shirt and a light fleece.

Seeing Natalia in the hotel reception, Betts took Natalia's arm and led her out into the sunlight. Neither of them were in the mood for conversation as they turned the corner to the heart of Old Portsmouth. Natalia still wondered where they were heading for. Betts indicated to the Cathedral which had risen up in front of them.

"We're in here," he said, "the home of the UK operation."

So Portsmouth Cathedral was to be the venue for her meeting. Momentarily, she thought it strange that this historic property served as the location for what had to be undertaken. What a place to act as a disguise for the realities of their trade! The authorities would be reluctant to disturb any comings and goings within the Cathedral itself, and generally all connected with this building would be seen as pillars within their community.

Betts and Natalia entered through the southern gate, arriving in the main body of the Cathedral with its lofty domed ceiling many metres above. They immediately turned right to follow the first flight of wide stone stairs which curved round to the landing, holding the body of the organ.

Up through the small, wooden door situated adjacent to the organ pipes that led to the ringing chamber itself, Natalia peeped through the narrow glazed window slits and was rewarded with a dusty view of part of the naval docks. The ringing chamber door opened at Betts's insistent push and both Natalia and the Petty Officer stepped down into the large, open room which appeared to have been built around the inner circle of levitating ringing ropes, tied in mid-air ready for the Sunday morning service.

CHAPTER 70

Crying himself to sleep, David had had a fitful night. He had been aware of the breathing of his two companions within the dark cellar room and had been unable to move from his spot by the door. He was rooted in position and had been, since arriving in the early hours of the morning, still dressed in his black tie from the ball the previous evening.

David truly was a sorry sight. He appeared to be empathising with the two captives. Their forms were dimly outlined against the wall, sleeping underneath their respective grey blankets on the two old bed frames across from David. If he had been able, he would have been sorely tempted to release his prisoners from their shackles, attached to each of the bed frames. But he was unable, and had to focus his attention to the money. Yes, the money, keep thinking about the money, he told himself; what he could do with it; how it would change his life; all the ways the money would benefit him and change his future. Taking care of these captives would feel like a slight hiccup in the overall scheme of things; a trial to test him. Come on David, if you cannot cope with this simple situation then do you really deserve all of those extra notes?

But was it worthwhile? What good was all this if he had lost the love of his life? What really was the love of his life? The girl? The money? The buzz of the adrenalin in doing a deal? His head ached from all of the different thoughts going around like a whirlwind.

What did he want? Where was he going to be in ten years? Well, forget that, how about in two or three years? No, it was not possible to think that far ahead. Let's be realistic. How about a half year tops, yes, a half year? David focused on the next six months of his life. He was dreaming of a beautiful motor yacht somewhere warm. The Caribbean would do, yes the Caribbean. He was surrounded by friends, some lovely ladies and a wonderful, beautiful, giggling girl with slightly curly hair, right by his side. She was laughing at the joke that he had just told. His humour had always been good. It reeled her in. Let's finish the wine, David was saying to the gorgeous and sexy and curvy lady, and then go for a dip in the sea. Her body language indicated that she could not wait. There was a loud rattle of the anchor chain, but it was not in David's dream. It was the here and now. Oh no, thought David, crushed again, back to reality. The reality of this pit of a hole that was once a cellar. The teenage daughter had just turned over and it had caused her ankle chain to rattle. David sighed; he would get out of this. He was not the type to give up. People had adored his company for his humour and companionship but, with money as well, he would be laughing.

CHAPTER 71

Archie woke with the dawn light, which shone in through the French balcony doors, direct in his face. The sofa had not been that comfortable but he had not required the use of it for anything other than sitting and slumping in, since buying the flat.

Wow, Emma was in the room next door lying in his bed and yes, in his bedroom. Right, softly, softly, he thought. He must not wake her. Archie had made up his mind. He had things to do, places to be, and was on a mission, literally. Although not having the support of Commander Edgar Bennett and the resources of the whole of Naval Command, Archie would not be put off the scent.

His mission to the Alps had turned everything around. All leads had pointed directly back to Portsmouth. The paper that Nick had found consisting of the historic ships pass and the half faded and scrawled address led to Portsmouth. Petty Officer Betts had turned up in Portsmouth. A complete shock but, nonetheless, the man was here and Archie had witnessed him talking to David of all people. Archie remembered that David had carried out some volunteering work as a guide on the historic ships but crossed his fingers that David and Betts' relationship did not extend further.

The van that had driven off hastily from the rear of the Student Union car park had contained copious amounts of perfectly separated, small packages. Archie was not a complete fool; he knew what they were, even if he did not know what was going on. How was David mixed up in this? How deep did he go?

Archie knew that he was one of the very few people that David had trusted enough to reveal that he had been brought up in a children's home. He realised that, despite having lived with David many years ago during their first year at University, he knew very little about him. What were his activities and hobbies apart from the obvious? The water-polo, hockey and other team sports were forever on display and Archie was now aware that David had continued to bell-ring at St. Mary's. However, Archie also recognised that he had lost track of the true David, and everything that he might be caught up in now.

Archie's brain was quickly jumping through different possibilities but all of them involved David. He needed to track David down. Archie was sure that he was at the heart of this mess. David would enable Archie to understand whatever was going on.

Archie wrote a note for Emma to pick up and left it on the sitting room table. He quietly let himself out of his flat and had the all important piece of paper in the back pocket of the blue jeans he was wearing. By walking to where David now lived, Archie would see if he could catch up with him at the hall of residence in the city centre.

It was quiet on this Sunday morning and there was little pedestrian or vehicular traffic at this early hour. Archie noticed a large, speeding Audi heading the other way, in the direction of the Cathedral. He checked to see if there were any other motorists before crossing the road towards the Guildhall and David's hall of residence, which lay opposite.

Entering the student accommodation by pressing the caretaker's buzzer, the only route was through to the reception. Archie was surprised to hear that David was not in and had to admit that he was temporarily stumped in the search for David. He asked the caretaker if he knew where he was and received a negative response. David's friends would not thank Archie for waking them up at this time in the morning, but Archie's business was urgent. He took the stairs two at a time to the second floor and it was only twenty seconds later before he arrived at the door of Richard Gupta. Back in the hall after the recent police visit, he was now answering every door knock and was on his best behaviour. Of course, Archie did not know that the student had been busted for his plant growing activities only weeks before, but even Richard did not have the faintest idea where David was. After a few second thoughts he said, "Try St. Mary's Church, he normally rings there first thing."

What Archie could not have known was that Emma had made her mind up in the early hours of the morning to support Archie in every possible way on his mission. Peering through the binoculars that she had borrowed from Archie's flat, which he used to take in the comings and goings of the Solent, she stood close to a pillar on the side of the Guildhall. She was still in her purple dress, topped off by Archie's fleece, and was now watching the entrance to the hall of residence. Her plan was to help Archie and follow him to where he was heading. She would do everything in her power to help avenge the deaths of his colleagues who had suffered out in the Alps, whilst Emma had been recovering from her night on the mountain. She would wait until Archie reappeared.

CHAPTER 72

Emma saw Archie appear from the entrance to David's hall of residence. He was in a rush and seemed slightly flustered, but had a sense of purpose and clearly knew where he was going.

Emma was nervous and excited, eagerly awaiting a hint as to where Archie was heading. Searching for David, she expected him to go to the Student Union, the engineering block or the library, though if he was not in his hall room, it was much too early for these other options on a Sunday morning. Perhaps he had just been given a tip off by a friend living in the hall?

Emma had to move quickly. She could not let Archie leave her sight, and he was walking at a pace. She could see the hunger in his stride and the yearning for closure. Her man had been troubled and he wanted to put his demons to rest.

Almost running to keep up, she had crossed the Guildhall Square and had passed the road which led to David's hall of residence. Archie was walking up towards north Portsmouth and Fratton, where Emma had never been before.

Filled with row upon row of nineteenth century terraced housing, north Portsmouth did not have the natural green areas of Southsea Common or the beauty of the open ocean. Much of the area had become run down and many of the houses were boarded up, with few facilities and very few professionals. Little inward investment had been attracted and this was what was direly needed.

Archie looked around him as he crossed to the other side of the road, past one of the few trees which was attempting to retain as much of its blossom as long as possible. The blossom only remained where it was out of reach of the local kids. Snapped off lower branches lay strewn around the base.

Emma had to dodge for cover behind a parked van and, when she was sure that Archie had continued on his way, she crossed the road and continued to follow him. She was nervous, excited and apprehensive. Where was Archie going?

Around the next corner taken by Archie, he walked onto St. Mary's street, leading to the partially dilapidated old church itself. It desperately needed repair work, and Emma noticed the temporary boarding where there seemed to have been a spate of recently smashed windows. Archie walked past the church and then abruptly stopped. Emma hid behind what appeared to be three abandoned wheelie bins.

Archie was ringing a door bell. She could see the outline of his head from the crack between the dark green wheelie bin and the black one, and it seemed as though he was standing on the doorstep for an eternity. There was no response.

Whilst Emma stayed put, Archie seemed to have disappeared around the corner, although something in his walk indicated to Emma that he was watching the house. The time dragged by. Emma was wondering what she was doing. It was still early in the day and fortunately there were not many people about. She reflected there was definitely no-one else wearing their ball clothes from the night before! The few birds in this part of Portsmouth were singing their morning chorus.

It all happened very quickly. So quickly in fact, that Emma just saw the back of David going into the house. Archie had reappeared, hiding behind a parked car on the opposite side of the street. So, Archie had tracked David down to a house in north Portsmouth. What was David doing here, Emma wondered? She knew that David lived in the hall of residence and had few other friends. She was sure that there were no other mature students in this part of town. Was it a bell-ringing friend?

Emma had met David when playing hockey and, whilst he had been fairly quiet about his campanology hobby, she had been intrigued by it. She only knew that he occasionally rang the bells at this church, and she thought that he had not been ringing for some time.

David had only popped back to the house. As quickly as he had appeared, he was turning the key in the lock and walking towards where Archie was hiding, with a small rucksack under his arm. Were Archie and David into whatever Archie had been talking about together? Had it all been a lie? Had Emma been totally and utterly fooled by this man who had swept her off her feet? She really, really hoped not.

Emma had to move from where she had been hiding for the last half an hour. She had to see where David was going to and keep an eye on Archie, who had moved along to some wilted bushes further along the road. David was not going far. He was looking around to see if he was being watched. He opened up a grate in the stone pavement outside the church. Then he disappeared.

Archie ran across from where he had been hiding. No sooner had Emma ducked than Archie was disappearing out of view also. She stood up from where she had been crouched and saw the half-closed paving slab. She put all rational thoughts to the back of her head and went to lift the stone cover.

CHAPTER 73

The paving slab was heavier than she thought, though not nearly the weight that it should have been, having been replaced by a lighter weight alternative and made to match the surrounding colours. Emma used both her hands and bent her knees to pull the slab open into the upright position. She let it clunk back down to the surface. It gave out a small thud as it landed on the stone path adjacent. Even from close proximity, it had fitted in extremely well. It was only when you lifted it that you realised the cover was much more recent than the other slabs.

Emma peered down and saw the vertical, shiny, metallic ladder leading to the base of the floor below. Archie and David were nowhere to be seen so Emma had no choice now. She just had to follow on. Descending the ladder into the gloom she did wonder if she was making the right decision.

From behind the thick wooden door immediately in front of her she could hear two voices in intense discussion. The voices were raised, the density of the materials within this subterranean layer blocked out most sound. The light was only partial but Emma's eyes were becoming more accustomed to her surroundings. Apart from the ladder which she had descended and the thick wooden door, there was nothing else to take in. Should she call the police? She attempted to make out what was being said by gluing her ear to the door but to no avail. The voices just produced muffled sounds and she recognised both.

Emma felt she had no choice. She pushed open the wooden door with all her weight and went into the underground chamber.

Emma found it difficult to take in what her eyes were telling her. Archie and David were both on their feet in front of her. Their conversation was more than animated, it was rapidly moving from being an intense discussion to pointing, gesturing, assertion and aggression. Down to her left was a covered chamber pot and to her right were two metal beds. Grey sheets covered the majority of the two occupants but their heads were both watching the events unfurling in the room. What were these two ladies doing here? Emma's presence stopped David and Archie in mid-flow.

As if in unison, David and Archie both looked at each other and asked pointedly, "What's she doing here?"

David added, "Archie, you've done enough by stealing Emma away, let alone come and follow me here. What is going on? Why is Emma with you?"

Emma was shaking as Archie and David started to push each other across the room. Their builds were very similar and the two of them were of equal height.

"Stop it!" she screamed.

This seemed to bring about a momentary pause in the jostling that was taking place.

"I said stop it!" Emma demanded in vain as David continued to push Archie back to the far wall. David worked himself up into a rage whilst pummelling Archie in the stomach, the ribs and the arms. He kept thumping him, an endless torrent of emotion. Archie attempted to block his blows and question him at the same time. Who was he working with? How did he know Betts? What were the two women doing in this underground chamber?

Archie was backed up against the far wall, and had nowhere to go. He attempted to take David's legs out from underneath him; to pin him on the ground so that he could be contained. However, David had other plans. The man was like an animal. David had resented the fact that Archie had come between him and Emma. He also resented Archie for his good looks, for his perfect life and for discovering David in the midst of his other life. How would he cover it up now? It was Archie who had brought Emma into it... and she had to see him in this mess also. Archie just could not be forgiven.

David clouted him on the jaw and Archie went down. David kicked him in the head, once, twice, another few times, violently, without mercy, out of control. Emma ran towards David to make him stop. In the small contained space she had not gained any momentum and David cast her to one side. Emma threw out her arms to protect herself from landing directly onto the hard floor. David loomed over her, grinning, and Archie lay next to her. He was not making a sound.

CHAPTER 74

Emma stared up at David, who was looming over her.

"Please don't hurt me," she said.

He laughed, "Do you really think I would ever want to hurt you, Emma? It's him that I have the problem with." As David spat out the words he kicked Archie again in the ribs. Ironically, he was lying in the recovery position.

Archie groaned as spittle ran from the corner of his mouth diagonally across the edge of his chin to form a pool on the floor. He started to emit a small trickle of blood along the same route.

"C'mon, you're coming with me," David said to Emma and reached down to grab her arm but Emma refused to cooperate.

"We can play this the easy way or the hard way, Emma. Please don't make me hurt anyone else in this room or hurt your lover boy even more."

Emma started to rise to her feet whilst David dragged Archie a yard closer to the metal frame of the bed with the teenage daughter lying on top. David produced a third leg chain and shackle from the darkness of the far corner of the room. Archie was only semi-conscious and not aware of David clicking the lock into place around his ankle and then securely padlocking the other end around the base of the bed-frame.

Emma appeared to have given up, standing hunched in the corner of this basement room, as far away as she could be from David.

David went over to Emma. He took her in, the hazy glow of a beautiful female form was now buried under an exterior of hate, fear and coldness. David looked closely into Emma's eyes. He touched her right arm gently; it was close to a caress. His left hand touched her cheek and drew a line down to her chin.

"Emma, did I ever tell you that I really like you, that I've liked you from the moment I first saw you at the hockey practice night. I recall all those times that we've had fun, that we have been lost in each other's company. We just need to forget that this ever happened. Can you do that? Can you do that for me?"

Emma was whimpering in the corner of the room but she was attempting to hold it together. She would attempt to use this whole situation to her advantage. If she could just hang in there, fight for what she was worth, fight for Archie and his downed colleagues. She pulled all her strength together to stay focused, to keep the end vision in her mind, to concentrate on what was being said. Had that really just been said? She was trying to hide her disgust and ignore Archie's shallow breaths and attempts at groans; to avoid any eye contact with the middle aged woman or the teenage daughter who had seen Emma and Archie as lifelines. She had seen the lights in their eyes. No-one could properly hide hope when it was as big as theirs.

David continued to speak, "Right, we're getting out of here, Emma. We've a meeting to attend and you're going to be safe with me. If you do anything stupid, then you're going to cause pain and suffering here, and if pretty boy attempts to escape, then you might want to be worried, Emma. Don't be worried for now though, I'm going to take care of you."

He pushed Emma up the metal loft ladder, having locked the heavy wooden door to the underground room behind him. Once on the surface, David replaced the paving slab to match the surroundings, then he took hold of Emma's hand slightly too firmly and they strode away from the church together.

If it was not for the wincing expression on Emma's face, everyone else that Sunday morning would have taken them for a hungover, young, student couple. The ball glad rags gave them away as students, and at this early hour of the morning it could only be assumed they were scurrying back to their own homes.

CHAPTER 75

Emma was being pulled along by David, in partial shock at what she had just witnessed. Her thoughts were confused. David was telling her to watch where she was going. How could she when she did not know where they were walking and, she was uncertain whether she wanted to go wherever she was being led.

It seemed futile to resist. David had over-powered Archie and the women in the underground room were reliant on David coming back to them. All she could do was take in the proceedings that she was unwillingly a part of, to allow her to be in the best possible position for whatever lay ahead.

David had picked up the pace and was virtually dragging her along. In order to avoid a scene, his voice was low and cold, but reminded Emma that she was directly influencing the welfare of the Woodcutter's wife and daughter, and of Archie. David reminded Emma that Archie needed medical help but he would only receive what he needed if she hurried up and did exactly what he said.

Skirting the university buildings, David and Emma passed by the Student Union, the library and one of the lecture halls. As the couple walked past the library, Emma willed there to be students looking out of the windows who might notice that she was walking with this man against her will. There were normally students looking out of the windows, straying from their studying. It was early but why were there not any students gazing in their direction today? Sod's law, she decided. Opportunity one was gone.

They were now walking on the cobbled pavements of Old

Portsmouth and about to pass a couple of the oldest pubs in the town. The Duke of Nelson was flying its colourful flag, enticing passers-by into its restful interior. The flag provided a marked contrast to the black and white of the exterior dark wooden beams with the whitewashed plasterwork in between. There were more people about and David whispered a word of caution to Emma, "If you say anything," he muttered, "they will be hurt."

Emma refrained from making a show of her predicament. She did not know what to do. She felt like a rabbit in the headlights. Keep thinking, Emma told herself. There had to be a way round her current situation. Nothing was obvious so, for the moment, she would have to continue being an unwilling pawn for a while longer.

The Cathedral loomed ahead and Emma was surprised when David drew Emma closely to him. "Now Emma, you are going to follow me and pretend to be a part of a wonderful and loving Christian couple." He giggled at Emma's look of pain and kissed her tenderly on the side of the cheek.

As they approached the Cathedral side path he clasped her hand more tightly. The daffodils were coming out in the manicured lawned areas on either side of the walkway, with their strong yellow buds forcing themselves out of the tall green shoots. Emma and David arrived at the body of the Cathedral itself. David opened the side door which led directly into the main nave and stepped to one side for Emma to walk through.

David walked Emma up the wide stone staircase situated to the side of the body of the Cathedral, close to the main entrance. They turned an immediate left at the top of the stairs and went slowly past the organ. The organist was due to be stroking the ivory keys of the fine instrument in the next thirty minutes and David did not want to disturb him as he was going through his music books. David softly pushed open the small, wooden door that led to the ringing chamber, and let Emma climb up the small stone staircase in front of him.

CHAPTER 76

David led Emma up the steep and narrow stone steps to the ringing chamber. She had never entered a ringing chamber before and, whilst visibly nervous, it was clear that Emma was taking everything in.

In stepping onto the wooden panelled floor she noticed the ringing mats underneath each of the tied and hanging bell ropes. The bell ropes formed a perfect circle with the tail ends tied up around the main body of the ropes, just below the fluffy sally. They were bright and colourful, in stark contrast to Emma at this moment. They consisted of concentric bands of white, blue and red. The colours were just the personal preference of the tower and were not significant.

To her left was the great tower clock, protected in its case. The case was made up of an outer box of wood, which rose from the floor to an average person's shoulder height, and this was topped off with glass panels that allowed you to see the intricate workings of the mechanical dials, cogs and metallic arms within.

On the walls were the numerous peal boards. These large, wooden plaques reminded Emma of the grave stones below. They listed the name of a method with the last word of the method telling you how many bells the peal had been rung on. So major would mean eight bells, caters indicated nine bells and royal ten bells. The boards also detailed if the heaviest bell, the tenor, was involved and moving about, or if it continuously 'donged' at the back whilst the other bells changed their order. Below the method name were listed the participants in order from the treble to the tenor. A small 'c' by the name would mark the caller or captain who had been in control of the ringing.

Emma was staggered at the history of the place. She knew she was in a Cathedral but she did not expect there to be peal boards going back to the nineteenth century and David was letting her know that many peals had been rung before then.

There were countless shelves of ringing books and resources, some which would benefit from a dust, she thought, and some more recent pictures of the current ringers on outings, at meetings and for general gatherings consisting of meals and drinking. She was surprised that there were so many social pictures outside of the tower that involved drinking, but reflected that wherever you had a ringing tower, you probably had a very good pub.

Emma was surprised that no-one else was around. She was aware that the service was due to start in the next half an hour, she had noticed the organist preparing himself, and knew that the bells were rung before and after the service. David indicated to Emma to climb the vertical ladder that led to the bell chamber.

"Why?" said Emma.

"We just have to see the views on this lovely spring day," David replied.

Actually interested by the prospect of how the bells would appear in the bell chamber and the far reaching views that must be possible from the top of the tower, Emma started to climb the steep wooden steps that led to the bells above. She could not shake the thought of Archie and the two women in the underground chamber from her mind, but perhaps the views would do her some good, and allow her to think of a way out of her current situation.

The large, red, metal bell frame appeared to her left. The bells had been completely renovated for the Millennium and were still going strong. The ten bells were arranged in a tightly

212

squeezed fashion with the tenor directly ahead of her under the ladder leading to the tower roof and the two trebles, tiny by comparison to her immediate left. The bell chamber was dark compared to the brightness of the ringing room below and the shuttered louvers on each side of the tower were partially closed to limit the amount of noise heard from the outside. This soundproofing worked to good effect and meant that, as long as the ringers continued to ring at the allocated times, and to a reasonable standard, there would be few complaints.

Emma reached the trapdoor that opened to the tower roof and looked down towards David. David told her to push it upwards, close to the catch which she had just released. The trap door sprung open into the upright position so that Emma and David could jump up onto the tower roof. The sun seemed to shine directly towards Emma and David as they pushed themselves up to a standing position.

However Emma felt ambushed and that the sun was not shining on her. Surrounding her on the roof was a Spanish-looking lady in a smart trouser suit and dark hair. She seemed to be with an athletically built, middle-aged man in blue jeans and a shirt. Standing next to the Spanish lady was an older, slightly pot bellied, businessman who gave the manner of being the leader of the group, with a similarly mature lady adjacent to him with whitish hair. Lastly, next to the lady with whitish hair was a hulk of a man, who gave off a strong military demeanour and wore an overcoat and deer stalker hat. Despite the sun shining, it was still cool so the hat gave his short hair a helping hand to keep his head warm.

All eyes immediately turned their focus to Emma, making the chilly morning air the least of her concerns.

CHAPTER 77

"Ah," said the Tower Captain as Emma reached the roof, "one of our spies." There was a look of agreement amongst the group, akin to the impression that Emma was the scum of the earth. She was being viewed as though she were something that you had trodden in, and wanted to be rid of. Their faces indicated that she needed to be dealt with.

Emma did not know what the Tower Captain was talking about. "One of your spies, what do you mean?" the words came out with a lack of confidence and conviction, even though Emma was deeply trying to hold it together. She was in turmoil and rapidly succumbing to the shock of her roof top welcome.

"You have been spying on our operation," the Tower Captain said. "You and your friend Archie." Emma now began to comprehend where the misunderstanding lay. "No…" she began, "I've only just got to know Archie, I know nothing of what you do."

"Well, we cannot take that risk" the Tower Captain said with an air of finality and indicated to David and the Woodcutter and Betts to deal with the matter. The Tower Captain descended with Natalia and Mavis to the meeting room adjacent to the ringing chamber below.

Whatever Emma had imagined, the final position that she found herself in was ultimately far worse.

The Woodcutter and Betts had told David to go downstairs to join the Tower Captain and the others, and stay out of sight. David clearly still had feelings for Emma but could only have decided now that she was past redemption and left Betts and the Woodcutter to carry on with their work.

Betts looked on with glee, he immediately pinned Emma's hands behind her back and laughed, "Are we going to have some fun with you," he gloated. Within ten minutes, having forced Emma down to the bell chamber, Betts had held up his piece de resistance. An old jacket like contraption. Emma did not recognise what it was but the clothing had come from the man's ex-military equipment.

They forced her arms inside the sleeves and around her front so that they were crossing each other. Her hands had to squeeze closed inside the material so that all her fingers were touching, and then were pulled extremely tightly towards her back. Her right arm wrapped round to her left and her left arm wrapped round to her right. They forced a strap adjoined to the jacket around her neck and one from her waist between her legs to a buckle on her back, and tightened the contraption. Betts wove rope around her ankles and knees, and gagged her with part of an old bell rope. Betts had already doused the old bell rope in chloroform otherwise Emma would not stay still enough for what Betts and the Woodcutter were about to do.

Emma could not move at all and was extremely scared. She was not expecting any of this and the rope gag had sent Emma into muffled screams for a few seconds before the chemical did its work. The tenor bell was in the upside down position, the wooden slider balancing against the stay. The stay appeared extremely fragile and Betts highlighted to the Woodcutter that the Tower Captain had already carried out a neat job of sawing through three quarters of the stay. The next pull, involving the bell slider hitting the stay, would be enough to send it crashing through.

Emma was hoisted up into the air by both Betts and the Woodcutter and gently placed inside the upturned bell. She was wedged around the clapper to the side of the bell that leant onto the stay. "I wouldn't move, if I were you Emma, as you wouldn't want to come crashing down on us, would you?" Betts laughed in an excited manner, as though he could not wait for it to happen.

Emma was totally unaware of her predicament as she had passed out into a deep sleep. She could not begin to comprehend that if the bell was allowed to crash through the wooden stay that balanced the one ton chunk of metal currently held upside down, it would keep dangerously swinging back and forwards. The weight of the bell would continue to make it swing to and fro under its own momentum until it had released all of its energy and gravity had pulled it down to a standstill.

Emma would not know what would happen to her. Would she fall out as a dead weight to the bell chamber floor, or would the speed of the swinging with her being wedged to the side of the clapper hold her in to the sides? She would have to focus on anything else, something that would provide her with hope. Try as she might, no immediate thoughts would come to mind. Everything tangible that she would think of – Archie, the women – just brought her closer to despair.

CHAPTER 78

Betts and the Woodcutter lowered themselves to join Mavis, the Tower Captain, Natalia and David, who had all already descended the belfry ladders and walked across to the meeting room adjoining the ringing chamber.

Both Betts and the Woodcutter were surprised by the number of individuals in the room. Gathered together were a mixed group of people who were mostly in their late middle age. Betts and the Woodcutter took in the greying hair, the hands adjusting spectacles, the audience locating their seats for the meeting. Above all, there was the constant shuffling of impatience which pervaded the assembled throng.

You could also feel that a clear excitement hung in the air about being within the gathered number, within this seemingly select group. The two men viewed every person from the entrance door located at a ninety degree angle to the layout of the room. They noticed the top table facing the chairs, the only furnishings of the room, and all of the attendees who were very ready for the meeting to begin.

Betts and the Woodcutter took the empty couple of seats nearest to the door and waited attentively for the Portsmouth Cathedral Tower Captain to begin. The Tower Captain stood up from behind the centre of the top table. He was a man who naturally held an audience captive as he had an air of authority. His mannerisms intrigued and fascinated and left you wanting more. Confident, assertive and projecting the cut and thrust of what they were all here for. How much money were they going to make? When would they receive it? What would they all have to do to ensure the utmost secrecy and that the supply reached all the necessary parts of the country?

The group had come together from far and wide with Tower Captains persuaded to come on board from all parts of the United Kingdom. These regional area representatives would store the supply easily within their towers and the storage was discreet. Whoever checked belfries, ringing chambers and other areas within towers apart from the ringers themselves? The first trial of the system had worked well. So well that the supply was to increase fivefold. The stock on the *Islander* would cover the pensions of all in the room with money to spare.

The Spanish lady with the dark hair stood up and oozed annoyance. She took the assembled party through how the cocaine was put together as a paste in the jungle rainforest. How she received the packages in Lima once they had travelled across the barren heights of Bolivia by 4x4 vehicle; the onward route by llama trains over the Andes through to the warehouses of the sea port. She reiterated the blood, sweat and tears sacrificed for the supply. She took her rapt audience through the loss of life on this trip alone, the reduced number of packages provided by the original tribal people due to issues with Government forces in Bolivia. She demanded more money for the supply otherwise none of those present would be receiving any cut whatsoever. Natalia returned to her seat having shocked those listening into a deadly silence.

The organ started to play in the distant body of the Cathedral. It signalled that there were only fifteen minutes to the morning service and then the joyous sound of the bells would peal out. The bells would wake those who were snoozing and reminded the remainder that Sunday had truly begun.

The Tower Captain's face was pale. Normally a larger than life character, this was most unusual. His face had completely drained of blood, leaving him appearing slightly nauseous.

His other half, Mavis, put her hand on his forearm, pinching him gently between her finger and thumb. He seemed to come round out of his ghost like trance. "Yes, we will increase your fee, Natalia, but we need to see the stock first. It is imperative that it is distributed successfully to all gathered here. This is only fair."

Natalia was not in a position to argue. Without her brothers acting as her personal henchmen she would have to employ others to carry out any physical work that was required. She accepted the Tower Captain's words, and the whole mood of the room lifted. The Tower Captain and Natalia completed pre-prepared draft documentation that would be fully agreed once the stock had been tested by the Tower Captain's organisation. Natalia commented that, as the first stage of business had been completed, she would be on her way.

With that, all the eyes of the room watched carefully as Natalia confidently left the room, as discreetly and swiftly as she had arrived. Betts quickly made his excuses and dashed out behind her and all those within the meeting returned to the multitude of queries regarding how the supply routes would work and when each of them would receive their proportion of the stock.

CHAPTER 79

The meeting drew to a close and David was impressed by how the Tower Captain had run the operation. All of the members of their small and select group knew what they were doing. Secrecy had been maintained. There did not appear to be any signs of issues with the authorities. David had taken care of Archie, and Emma had been taken care of by Betts and the Woodcutter, albeit David did not want to know what had happened to her.

David had been surprised by how quickly the Spanish lady had come and gone but reflected that was how she functioned. Efficient, clinical, unemotional and ruthless. Betts had clearly fallen for her, and had not been able to disguise his need to chase after her. It was clear to David that Betts wanted to get to know her much better prior to her return to South America.

After all of the other representatives had left, the Tower Captain went to a small cupboard that was discreetly located behind the top table. The Woodcutter and David had not noticed it during the meeting. Soon the chinking and clinking sound and the wry smile on the Tower Captain's face indicated that he was about to offer something special. The cupboard door opened to reveal an old Wade Bell's Scotch whisky decanter full of the spirit distilled and blended in Perth, Scotland. He proffered the Bell's whisky to Mavis, David, and the Woodcutter, and sat back in his chair, savouring the taste from his own beautiful cut glass tumbler.

The Woodcutter was congratulated on his management of the operation in the Alps, even though it was clear that the authorities were on their tails. His swift departure and evacuation of the chalet and the successful infiltration of the government mission by Betts, had meant that all was still on track.

The Woodcutter had not drunk any of his whisky and instead was pointedly staring directly into the eyes of the Tower Captain. He could not keep his silence any longer. "Where is my family?" he spoke calmly. "I have to see my wife and daughter now. You have paid me for what I have done for the survival of your operation, but I need to be reunited with my family."

The Tower Captain took the Woodcutter to one side and started to explain that he had one last mission for him and then the Tower Captain would reveal exactly where his wife and daughter were. He threw two sets of keys towards the Woodcutter, who looked confused. Clearly, the Woodcutter did not know that the keys had the power to open the solid wooden door to the underground chamber and also open the locks connecting the ankle chains to the bed frames occupied by his wife and daughter.

The Tower Captain and the Woodcutter heatedly discussed whatever this last mission was, with Mavis and David looking on. It appeared to David that whatever the Tower Captain was saying, it was causing the Woodcutter difficulty. Both of the men were gesticulating and, whilst trying to keep their voices low, rapid sentences were flying from each of their mouths.

Finally, they appeared to come to some form of agreement with the Tower Captain giving the Woodcutter some form of directions. The Tower Captain gave the Woodcutter a hard slap on his back and then said, "So long, I will hear from you within the next hour when you have done the deed. The event will be clear enough from the tower roof so that I can direct you to your family who are in perfect health, isn't that right David?" the Tower Captain called over.

David dropped his head towards the floor as he could not look at the Woodcutter. The Tower Captain had told him to have some form of protection if the Woodcutter caused trouble, but David was not bothered with that. He could take care of himself.

David at last raised his gaze, "Yes," David replied. "They are both in perfect health."

CHAPTER 80

Betts had raced out of the tower after Natalia. Running as quickly as he could down the never ending curving tower steps, along the organ balcony and then hopping over the wider steps that took him into the body of the Cathedral and through to the main doors, the sunlight suddenly streamed into his eyes. He had not appreciated the relative darkness within the building itself. There she was, dark hair bobbing along and nearly back on the road that led to Southsea Common.

Betts quickened his pace. It was not time to lose her now. Out of breath he caught up with Natalia. She turned towards him as he tapped her on the shoulder and looked deeply into those unfathomable auburn eyes, the stubborn yet beautiful face, the perfectly presented figure in the neat trouser suit.

Natalia did not want to be stopped or held up. She needed to return to her remaining family in Lima as the Tower Captain would confirm completion of the deal electronically, once the stock had been tested. "What do you want?" she snarled at Betts.

"I'll give you a lift to your hotel, and then to the airport for your flight," he said, as noncommittally as possible. "OK," she said, surprisingly without any hesitation. Natalia used people and was used to using people. This would save her a little time, she thought.

Natalia and Betts jumped into his rickety second-hand white van, in which he had originally picked her up. He crunched the gears, attempted a three point turn on the too narrow street, and on the fourth turn whisked them both towards Natalia's grand, seafront hotel. It was a short journey in the van and Natalia did not need long to freshen up, change and grab her things. After checking out of her hotel, Betts would then drive her to Heathrow airport for the flight to Lima in Peru, which stopped en-route at Rio de Janeiro.

Betts had kept the engine running. The chugging of the motor and the newspaper he was reading made him oblivious to the Woodcutter's movements underneath and behind the van. The Woodcutter had easily been able to follow Betts' movements in the van and had only needed to jog the couple of streets between the Cathedral and the seafront hotel to carry out his work.

If Betts was thinking anything, it was the thought of how he was to ensure that Natalia had a good send off; a parting that she would never forget. It might even ensure she returned to the UK one day to see how her trusted ally, Petty Officer Betts, was doing.

Natalia was up in her hotel room and thought that she might as well give Betts one last treat. He had been vital to their operation after all and could be very useful in the future to ensure that the Tower Captain did what he was told. Natalia picked out her belt like skirt and appropriate expensive lingerie. She did what she needed to be noticed, yet she wore it all with an air of sophistication, the distant attitude, the playing hard to get. It all just meant people found her more of a challenge; a special enigma which made it difficult to unravel the outer layers of her bravado.

Betts was not quite drooling as he loaded Natalia's two bags into the back of the van and opened the side door for her to hoist herself in, but he was not far from that state. This reaction reinforced Natalia's contention that men were like dogs. For dogs were creatures that were always after affection, naturally far too obvious with their feelings and generally loyal if you kept them fed and watered and gave them somewhere to stay.

Once away from the hotel, Betts accelerated and drove straight over the couple of mini-roundabouts that led them past the naval dockyard and the university buildings to the beginning of the M275. The motorway would take the little white van off the Isle of Portsmouth.

Unfortunately for them, the remains of Betts and Natalia would forever lie on the Isle of Portsmouth. As the van hit fifty miles per hour, it exploded into a spectacular fireball, the debris flying across the road and hitting oncoming vehicles in their path. There was immediate pandemonium within the vicinity.

As he gazed through his binoculars from the roof of the nearest, highest building, which happened to be a vacant office block, the Woodcutter reflected that Betts and Natalia would not have had time to know what had hit them, or more importantly, to have felt any pain. They would stay together forever, just as Betts had wanted.

The Tower Captain took in the scene in the far distance through his own eyes. His organisation had been able to test the quality of the stock immediately after the meeting and provide the Woodcutter his instructions to kill Natalia. The traffic was already backing up, sirens could be heard from vehicles making their way to the scene, and the noise of the explosion had been audible across most of the city. The Tower Captain gave the Woodcutter a call.

True to his word now that the deed had been done, the Tower Captain disclosed to the Woodcutter the location of his wife and daughter.

CHAPTER 81

The Woodcutter ran to the location that he had been given. He practically threw the surface chamber cover to one side, let himself drop to the bottom of the steel ladder and burst through the huge, wooden door, having used his first set of keys in the main lock.

He broke down in tears as he was reunited with his loved ones. His crying eyes became inflamed when he saw the ankle chains leading to the bed-frames. His urgency to remove them meant that the Woodcutter had not even noticed the body of the young man lying on the floor. He had almost tripped over the dark shape whilst reaching his family lying on the beds against the hard, cold, rear wall.

Hugging, touching, kissing his loved ones. They were all experiencing waves of emotion. Relief. They needed to be away, out. To breathe in the fresh air outside and above ground. They would take in the comings and goings of Portsmouth waking up, the people leisurely enjoying their Sunday morning strolls, walking dogs, buying newspapers.

The hump of the dark shape on the floor shifted, groaned. What was this? The Woodcutter furrowed his brow and scratched the back of his head. Who was this man? Had he been there all along? Where had he come from? The Woodcutter turned him over onto his back. In the pale light, it was not immediately apparent that the Woodcutter had met the Lieutenant before.

The Woodcutter's priority was to rescue his family. Having found them and now aware that they were both going to be alright, he wanted them all to be out of this underground pit as quickly as possible. He slapped the man a couple of times on the cheeks and he seemed to respond through further grunts and groans. The teenage daughter indicated the water and cups close to the wall and one of the cups full of water was proffered to Archie's lips. It only took a few seconds before there was any reaction. The man seemed to come round. He was battered and bruised. The Woodcutter could see that he had been repeatedly punched but he was definitely savouring the liquid. His energy had not diminished. He was presumably just in shock at being knocked out by someone and, it appeared, very recently.

It dawned on the Woodcutter who had control of this underground cellar, seeing that he had been given the keys from the Tower Captain, and who worked directly for the Tower Captain. The Woodcutter had had no direct contact with David, but from the few hours that he had spent with him during the morning he would not have trusted him as far as he could spit.

The Woodcutter's thoughts whirred into action. He realised that David had left this man on the floor in an injured state. The young man was now starting to move forcefully, to stretch out all of his limbs and shakily rise to his feet. Disorientated, on first attempt he careered off in the direction of the solid wall near the entrance and the chamber pot. Pulling himself together and standing still, leaning against the wall, he seemed to come round completely.

The Woodcutter appraised the man now that he was on his feet and had to swallow hard. It was more than a likeness. He had seen him before. Most people would not be too concerned if they had seen somebody before, but this was always worrying for the Woodcutter. Fortunately, it came to him where he had seen him previously, and this did not help his position any further. His memory had served him well, but had the man recognised him? If he had not already, it was just a matter of time. Well, he and his family would be out of here and long gone. The Woodcutter thought hard. This was a real opportunity. A chance for payback. He had always believed that what comes around, goes around.

The Woodcutter went over to Archie. He carefully gave him some more water, some chocolate and looked at him hard in the face, man to man. Archie had to concentrate. He was unable to see anything except this athletic torso of a man with military bearing and his overcoat and hat, which lay on the side of the bed. Oh no, thought Archie at the same instance, for he had clicked exactly who this hulk of a man was.

The Woodcutter saw the glimmer of recognition in Archie's eyes and started immediately to explain what he was doing and crucially, what he had been doing out in the Alps. The Woodcutter had his money. More importantly, he had his family. What did he have to lose?

CHAPTER 82

The bells would be ringing out at the close of the Sunday morning service. Archie was at least a fifteen minute jog away and could only concentrate on reaching the Cathedral in time to save Emma.

The Woodcutter and his family had departed from the underground cellar in haste once his wife and daughter and Archie's ankle shackles had been unlocked. The family would find a new life for themselves where they could settle down away from his military and special operations past. The money that the Woodcutter had earned promised a trouble-free future existence. In return for his slipping away, Archie had been given the information he needed to pursue the leaders of the operation, now that Betts and the South American lady had been blown away.

Archie similarly rushed out as quickly as the heavy wooden door, and the modern new metal ladder opening into the bright sunlight of this spring day, would allow.

This was it. It was his chance to bring to justice all those who had haunted him over the previous months. The departure of the Woodcutter was a small price to pay for the information he had provided. The details would enable Archie to capture the big cheese. The man responsible for the whole set up. The Cathedral was the centre of their drug running operation, and Archie now had the knowledge and power to destroy the entire supply and distribution network. The rug would be pulled from under the feet of the operation and send the participants' expected rewards toppling back down to earth. He could not believe the circumstances in which he found himself. Having known the Tower Captain and rung the bells so closely with him, the answer to all of his queries, to his previous entire mission, had lain right in front of his eyes.

Archie picked up his pace. This is what he had trained for. He used his mobile whilst on the run to make a couple of requests and, only slightly out of breath, continued as fast as he could with Emma pervading his every thought.

Over the next five minutes, his mind lay confused and racked with guilt. If he had not met Emma then she would not be in any danger. If he had not met Emma, he did not think that he would be feeling this concerned for anyone else. Since the chance meeting on the mountain and having talked all through the night after the Student Ball, he felt drawn to Emma in a way that he had never felt about anyone else. He did not like the cliché that they were destined for each other, but however hard it would be, whatever trial Archie had to undertake, he would do everything he could for Emma, even if it was not enough.

The tower of the Cathedral still lay a few hundred metres further on and Archie's heart was pounding through his chest. His shirt was clammy and starting to stick to his upper back. He was sweating profusely and his muscles ached.

Archie felt sick, even slightly dizzy and he started to despair as he heard the six smallest bells being raised in peal. What was going on? The Woodcutter had indicated that Emma had been dumped in an upturned bell and yet Archie was hearing the front six bells starting to ring. Think, Archie, think, he repeated to himself. If the bells had been lowered from a wedding the previous day then all of the bells would need to be rung up. Sometimes, the heaviest four would be left 'up', balanced against their stays. It was much more of an effort to ring them up and down and a human being would only fit into the tenor or, at a push, the ninth. The smaller bells were half way through the raise and it was a beautiful distinctive sound. Mavis would be on the treble, the Tower Captain would be on the tenor of the six and would soon ring the tenor of the full ring. Oh no, thought Archie, that was it. The Tower Captain himself would be sending Emma to her doom and Archie would not be able to stop it. Unless…

Archie was running in through the small exterior grounds of the Cathedral. The grappling ropes were in place. Jackie and Jo had already done their work and Jackie raised a hand to Archie from the top of the tower. Archie whisked himself up. He tried to ignore the bells ringing, the incredulous looks of a couple of passers-by as this young man hauled himself up the outside of the Cathedral tower using a couple of climbing ropes. What was he doing? Was this allowed?

The bells were starting to slow down and audibly separate into a uniform rhythm and speed. This was concerning. There was not long left until the back bells, which did not need ringing up, would start to ring out in glorious peal as part of the full set of ten.

Jackie and Jo had made light work of the tower hatch and were descending into the bell chamber. Archie had finally reached the top of the tower, hauled himself over the balustrade and dashed to the belfry opening to catch up with his operational team members. The girls had stopped. They did not know what to do. They had never been into a belfry before and were completely deafened. Slightly below them the six smaller bells were continuing to whirl around the space, with the larger four bells balanced upside down immediately to their right. If the larger bells moved even an inch, the girls would be in trouble. Archie made it clear that they needed to stay put. He desperately searched for Emma.

Frantically he peered inside the second largest bell, the ninth. Emma was not there. If she was screaming, Archie realised, he would not have heard her. He frantically balanced his feet sideways onto the main beam and went over to the tenor bell. He hopped up onto the frame and peered down into the inside of the bell. There she was. Terrified and unable to move. What had they done to her? A cramped and restricted body with ringing rope round her mouth, a dirty jacket clamping her arms around her torso and additional rope around her legs.

Archie was totally aware of the peril that Emma was in. The six lighter bells were now fully upright, but the ringers below in the ringing chamber continued to ring them. Just a little longer, Archie thought, give me just a little longer. Jackie and Jo would have to help remove Emma from her peril. Archie wedged a metal bar against the partially broken stay so that Emma could be dragged out of the upturned bell. Even though the metal was in place, it would only take a ringer below to pull the bell rope and all of them could say goodbye to their lives. The drugged Emma did not seem to react at first. Completely deafened by the bells moving and striking around her she did not gauge that she was being helped out until Archie, Jackie and Jo all heaved her to the side of the bell chamber. There was no time to say anything; all of their words disappeared into the din of the belfry anyway.

The girls concentrated on removing the metal that had been propped against the partially broken wooden stay and then, as had been discussed with Archie, quickly went to work on the stay of the ninth. Hacked successfully, the ninth bell would also crash through what was left of the wooden stay, and mean the bell would not stop turning until gravity brought its movement to a halt.

Archie ran up to the top of the tower, abseiled down the entire height of the Cathedral, sprinted round to the internal staircase that led to the ringing chamber door past the organ, took the narrow stone steps two at a time, pushed open the

232

door and descended into the ringing room. As all was quiet he said, in out of breath gasps to those gathered, but mainly in the direction of the Tower Captain, "Sorry I'm late. I don't mind ringing the tenor as a forfeit if you want to take the ninth…"

CHAPTER 83

David was standing in the ringing room of the Cathedral having helped to ring up the smaller front six bells with the local band. The local band had included the Tower Captain and Mavis and another of Archie's ringing mentors Richard. The Tower Captain felt gobsmacked when a noticeably bruised Archie walked into the ringing room, as it was only in the previous hour that David himself had made sure that Archie was secure within the underground room.

The Tower Captain responded quickly and hid his excitement. David recognised that this suggestion by a 'beaten up' Archie fitted well within their overall scheme. David played along. By Archie taking the tenor, Archie would pull the bell that would knock Emma into oblivion above. The irony was exquisite, and not lost on David. It would be a fitting, and hopefully final, ending for them both. The action of pulling the tenor rope was likely to do much more than Archie would normally expect. At the very least he would knock himself unconscious and escape with a minor injury and at worst he had a good chance of never ringing or doing any activity ever again. Perhaps it would be a slow death; David mused.

As the bell crashed through the wooden stay the rope would wrap up into the ringing chamber ceiling, the tail end of which Archie would be holding. It would happen so quickly that Archie would be off his feet and hitting his head on the ceiling joists, probably before realising he should have let go.

The Tower Captain nodded to Archie. This signal of

confirmation was enough to say that it was alright for Archie to take the tenor. Archie and the Tower Captain were to begin the most memorable ring of their lives. The Tower Captain wanted the tenor bell to be involved and moving about in the method and therefore shouted, "Right, a half course of Yorkshire Royal."

If they all pulled together as a band, the ringers knew that the method had the potential to sound very musical, to ripple along, and produce a beautiful ring.

Archie was concentrating as intensely as he had concentrated during any previous mission. Having saved Emma from her certain fate, he now had to ensure that he did not allow his bell to touch the stay. The crucial part would be when the method came to an end and all the ringers would have to stand their bells to stop them swinging and bring the reverberations of sound and movement of rope and ringer and bell to an end. If Archie allowed his bell to touch its stay with the normal amount of force, it would be certain to break through the weakened piece of wood.

The Yorkshire Royal sounded like a set piece. Archie, the Tower Captain, Mavis and David were all engrossed in their own thoughts. David and the Tower Captain could not help but glance at Archie every so often out of the corner of their eyes, this would be the end to all the spying and to any risk that lay in the way of their future fortunes. All the work that had taken place to ensure the smooth operation from South America and across the UK would now be worthwhile.

Everyone in the ringing chamber felt part of a special piece of bell-ringing. It was the build up to greater things. The type of experience that you want to go on and on and on. When it does come to an end you want to share what you have felt during the event. For David, the Tower Captain and Mavis, they could not share why this was such a special ring for them. Each of those in the know were ringing as if there was no tomorrow, totally absorbed and entwined within the moment, aware that they were on the edge of much more exciting and enriched lives.

The half course was nearly up and the Tower Captain was brimming with anticipation. He did not often feel how he felt at this moment and it was definitely not possible for him to put the experience into words. He knew that the band were less than a minute away from removing Archie permanently. He kept telling himself to concentrate and finally shouted "Plain Hunt," which would bring the ringers back into rounds within the next few moments.

Archie knew that he had to bring his bell to a stop and rest it exactly on the balance without letting it touch the stay. He was nervous. His thoughts remained on Emma. She would ensure that he could cope with this. His operation would rightfully succeed. The perpetrators would be brought to justice, with only a few seconds to go now. The Yorkshire Royal had come to a close, the band were ringing rounds, they were about to stand their bells.

CHAPTER 84

The Tower Captain shouted "Stand."

From call to actual action there is always a full motion of hand-stroke and back-stroke. At hand-stroke the ringers were holding onto the fluffy sally of their ropes whilst the remainder wrapped around the wooden wheels that powered the attached bells to swing. This was immediately followed by the back-stroke where all of the ropes dropped back down in sequence through the respective eye-holes in the ringing room ceiling. The length of the ropes fell down to the floor so that each ringer could then catch their fluffy blue, red and white sally to stand their bell.

As Archie, David, The Tower Captain and Mavis pulled their last back-strokes down before standing their bells at hand-stroke, there was a mixture of thoughts between them. Archie would do everything possible just to hold his bell on the balance so that he could pass the rope to someone else to allow him to check that Emma was really alright up above. David wanted to see Archie have a fitting end. If the bell did not drag him up by its rope to the ringing room ceiling and knock him out then David was going to see to it himself. The Tower Captain was well aware that Archie was just about to lose his footing, good riddance he thought. The lad had just come too close to upsetting the whole operation. Mavis, she had so many plans for spending, so many plans. She had not had a shopping expedition with her daughter Monica for ages. She would treat herself for the successful completion of the distribution of the stock from the *Islander*. Not a flashy shop, nothing ridiculous, just what she and her daughter deserved, a little luxury.

The bells started to stand in sequence, beginning with the lightest, the treble, which Mavis was ringing. She had the most time to take in what happened next. The time between the treble and all of the other bells standing was less than a second. The bells continued to stand at hand-stroke. Four, five, six. The wave of motion whipped round to the ninth which her husband was ringing.

He was not standing anymore; he was off his feet, being powered up to the ceiling by the rope. It happened so fast that he did not have time to speak or shout.

His head cracked against the rafters fifteen feet above before he tumbled to the floor. Out of control, falling head first downwards, he smashed into the polished oak floor boards with a deadly crunch.

Archie was still holding onto the sally. He had dared not move as he was balancing the whole weight of the tenor on the balance and knew the broken stay would not support the weight of the bell.

David rushed over to the crumpled body of the Tower Captain, who was soon surrounded by the rest of the ringers in the tower.

Archie managed to tap Richard with his outstretched right arm who had been ringing the eighth on the other side of the Tower Captain. Richard refocused on Archie who was still standing holding his rope, Archie pleaded with him,

"Can you ring the tenor down? There's no stay on this bell either and I need to phone for help and direct the ambulance crew up the tower."

At that moment, there were footsteps coming up the ringing chamber steps. What was he doing here? Archie could not believe it as Commander Edgar Bennett appeared.

CHAPTER 85

The Commander reviewed the scene that lay before his eyes. The Tower Captain appeared still, not moving and lying on the floor just off centre.

Most of the ringers were gathered around him, one checking for a pulse. Another, it was David, was holding his head and attempting to hear breathing or see his chest rise or fall. Archie, yes it was Archie, was scrambling up the ladder leading to the bell chamber. The Commander did not know that Archie was joining Jackie and Jo above to finally liberate Emma. A man was ringing down the lowest sounding bell, presumably the heaviest, in front of him, and the faces of all in the room were showing shock, strain and stress. They were in need for someone to take control.

The Commander was the man for the job. He called for calm. He organised the group of people to see if any had first aid experience. A couple had recently been on a refresher CPR course. "Get on with it then," said the Commander. The two ringers with the most resuscitation knowledge went to work. Once the Tower Captain had received air, the other ringer pressed down over his heart, pumping his lifeless chest in line with the numbers that he was counting, one through to fifteen. There was no reaction. They kept giving CPR, on and on. The ambulance crew had to be on site soon and take over but, in the meantime, the ringers did what they could.

David was in shock at having seen the Tower Captain hit his head and then crumple to the ringing chamber floor. The Tower Captain had been a father figure to him. Mavis was staring at David, almost crying, although she was not able to look at her husband lying on the floor of the ringing room, incapacitated and not responding to her fellow bell-ringers' attempts to bring him round.

Mavis eventually let the tears flood down her cheeks. The stream did not relent. On and on her tears flowed. She was crying for her dead husband, the Tower Captain, for her daughter Monica and how she would cope without a father and for David, the Tower Captain's honorary son.

The Tower Captain had always wanted a son and this had not been a part of their life together. When David came along as a student to the St. Mary's and Portsmouth Cathedral ringing group, the Tower Captain had wanted to get to know David. They became close. The Tower Captain had let David into their business venture. David was already dealing; but this was on a much larger scale. He had known that he could trust David, and the Tower Captain had been an important figurehead and mentor for him. Mavis continued to weep.

CHAPTER 86

The ambulance paramedics had an air of efficiency and training and appeared on the scene wearing their green overalls and took over from the two ringers who had attempted to revive the Tower Captain. Their local team was having a busy morning with their colleagues attending an accident on the M275. The authoritative voice of Commander Edgar Bennett subsequently ushered all of the ringers out of the tower and told them to wait at the bottom of the narrow stone steps.

This allowed the paramedics to go to work. Meanwhile, the Commander scaled the belfry ladder that continued up to the tower roof. At the top of the ladder the Commander had difficulty pushing open the hatch. The daylight streamed down towards him as he tilted his head upwards. He was greeted by Jo and Jackie who had stepped aside for Archie to talk with Emma.

Archie and Emma turned their attention towards the Commander.

"I was wrong," the Commander said simply to Archie. "We now have your man David downstairs, and it looks as though the ringleader has passed away. I've also had to surprise my personal assistant Monica, who was the daughter of the Tower Captain, as you probably already knew. They are both being led away from the Cathedral as we speak."

Archie viewed the Commander through fresh eyes. "I did not know about Monica and I am pleased that you caught David. Whilst we're unable to track down all of the South American suppliers, we've closed down this UK group for good." Archie's face lit up, all his worrying over the last few months might finally have come to an end.

"Fancy a walk," Archie said to all present.

It was on the seafront promenade that Emma and Archie, Jackie and Jo, and the Commander found themselves twenty minutes later. Wind blowing through their hair, the salt spray visible off the bow waves of the sailing yachts in the distance, all of the party took a moment to breathe in the air and absorb the far reaching horizon. The hovercraft was zooming across to Ryde on the Isle of Wight and the Pride of Bilbao ferry was making its way through the entry buoys. The ferry carefully kept the bobbing red buoys to the left and the green starboard buoys to the right. The ferry sea lane cut through this swathe of the Solent, leading all the way to the harbour entrance.

Not so many luxury cruise ships passed through Portsmouth anymore. When they did, the age old saying of "Port Out, Starboard Home" had significance if the occupants of the cabins wanted to have the view of the shoreline. These cabins were always the far more expensive quarters.

The Commander turned to Archie, "We need to catch up with all of the main stock that was brought off the *Islander*."

Archie nodded, for he had already had similar thoughts. "Let's take a trip up to the Tower Captain's place."

The five of them piled into the Commander's old Volvo and were soon off the Portsmouth roads and skirting through the southern Hampshire countryside. The outskirts of the town had given way to hedgerows, brambles and trees. The Commander wound down his window and rested a hand out onto the edge of the metal roof of the car.

The Volvo swept into the Tower Captain's grounds and up the long gravel drive to the beautiful old house. Archie had an intake of breath at the size of the property and Emma and the girls in the back savoured the perfectly manicured lawns and were peering as far as possible to the paddocks beyond.

What a place! It was impressive what drug money could buy. It took the five of them over thirty minutes to properly inspect the property and outbuildings. Emma had not been able to take her eyes off the pigs and hens. An incredible life, she considered. It was only once they had scoured the whole property that the car in the outbuildings and the other small packages in its boot were revealed to contain the remainder of the stock from the freighter; an incredible haul. The vehicle was full to the brim of cocaine, packaged in every way inside the metal chassis, which had been specially designed to take the sealed packages.

The Commander called in the Police and, once they had arrived, suggested that they all properly retire to the local public house, *The Bell Inn.*

"The property will have to go up for auction, you know Archie," said the Commander. "It would be a shame for a hard worker to miss out on such a beautiful rare opportunity, especially when that hard worker is still working in conjunction with the Navy, albeit discreetly, and would be at the top end of any previous officer scale."

Archie was stunned and could not keep his grin from showing. He had work to do, which included the lady opposite him. She was chatting away with Jackie and Jo, giggling at something that had amused them all, loving the scenery and surroundings and letting the countryside do much of the talking.

"I might just go for that auction, Commander, I might just do that." The five headed back up the lane by foot to the local hostelry. They could hear the police sirens closing in. Archie was warm inside and could not resist grabbing Emma's hand.

At last, Archie considered, life was definitely on the up.

EPILOGUE

Archie was humming to himself. He was digging over a vegetable bed, removing all of the weeds that had appeared over the previous wintry months. Many of the roots were extremely resistant to his pulling and levering. The local blackbird was singing in the tree above him and the nosy neighbourhood robin kept hopping forward and turning its head to an odd angle, checking to see if he had upturned any worms.

The young plants that Emma had grown from seed could shortly be planted. The seedlings had shot up in the greenhouse and were now thickening out ready to take their chances against any wild rabbits, rodents and general garden bugs.

Archie had extended the existing, traditional, vegetable patch to the house, by incorporating a couple of raised beds. He had also added fruit. The thin and wiry raspberry canes stood in front of one of the perimeter hedges, crisscrossed and internally dissected by the many blackberry brambles which led onto the gooseberry and blueberry bushes.

Archie turned towards the house, a good few hundred metres in the distance. Emma had appeared from the back door and she beckoned him in as lunch was ready.

What a life, Archie thought. Living in the house of his dreams with the girl of his dreams in a set up which he could only have imagined. Emma and Archie had become inseparable. Emma meant the world to Archie and everything they had been through over the last twelve months seemed insignificant compared to their current situation. The here and now was what he wanted to concentrate on. He had everything to live for. He put down his digging fork and garden gloves and walked over to the house, across the manicured lawns.

Emma appeared radiant. She had just been for a shower and had washed her hair, having started some internal decorating within the downstairs kitchen. She beamed as Archie approached. "I've something to tell you, Archie," Emma began. "Have you now?" Archie was unsure what was coming next but Emma pulled him into her arms "I love you, Archie!" she said. "Ahh!" responded Archie. He tickled Emma and then pulled her towards him further. "I love you too, Emma!"

Archie could not suppress his smile as Emma chuckled with her infectious giggle.

For more information, please visit:

www.greghunt.info
www.troubador.co.uk